The Undead Detective Agency

Book 1

Get It Together

Hiring
Call: XXX-338-8267

Shelby Rhodes

Copyright © 2022 by Shelby Rhodes

All rights reserved. No part of this publication may be reproduced, stored or transmitted in any form or by any means, electronic, mechanical, photocopying, recording, scanning, or otherwise without written permission from the publisher. It is illegal to copy this book, post it to a website, or distribute it by any other means without permission.

This novel is entirely a work of fiction. The names, characters and incidents portrayed in it are the work of the author's imagination. Any resemblance to actual persons, living or dead, events or localities is entirely coincidental.

Shelby Rhodes assert the moral right to be identified as the authors of this work.

Shelby Rhodes has no responsibility for the persistence or accuracy of URLs for external or third-party Internet Websites referred to in this publication and does not guarantee that any content on such Websites is, or will remain, accurate or appropriate.

Designations used by companies to distinguish their products are often claimed as trademarks. All brand names and product names used in this book and on its cover are trade names, service marks, trademarks and registered trademarks of their respective owners. The publishers and the book are not associated with any product or vendor mentioned in this book. None of the companies referenced within the book have endorsed the book.

First edition

Paperback ISBN number - 9798840870785

Editing: Emma Luna at Moonlight Author Service

Proofreading: Anita Ford

Cover Design: Shelby Rhodes

Bat Illustrations: Jahla D. Brown

Formatting: Emma Luna at Moonlight Author Service

CONTENTS

Blurb	vii
Author Note	viii
Prologue: Almost Ready?	1
1. The Call Of Fate	5
2. Interview With A Human	11
3. Tell Me Everything!	21
4. Test Drive To Our First Case	31
5. The Bat Slide—Breaking In As A Vampire 101	42
6. Ice Cream! Ice Cream! Chase?	53
7. Follow My Nose	62
8. Reapers	69
9. To Dumb Decisions	80
10. A Lack Of Communication	93
11. Understanding Octavius	104
12. Employee Rules	117
13. Mr. Sandman, Give Me A Break!	130
14. Is No One Normal?	141
15. Natural Enemies?	150
16. Passing The time	155
17. Got Yah!	165
18. The Case Of The Vanishing House	175
19. Everything Is Better With Glitter	186
20. To Horrible Ideas	194
21. Not A Ghost	201
22. A Witch's Diary	208
23. Choices In Worry	218
24. Simple Enough!	230
25. Round Two	236

26. Now What?	245
Epilogue: Off Again	254
About Shelby Rhodes	258
Follow Shelby Rhodes	259
Also by Shelby Rhodes	260

Blurb

Hello, there! I'm Octavius Evander. And this is the beginning of my story—well...sort of. It's not the very beginning. As a vampire, that story would be way too long to write down—think, before the Romans. Rather, this story is about how I met the love of my unlife. Okay, it will be mostly about the cool and fancy detective agency I opened and solving mysteries, but also a little about love too.

So, what does one need to open a detective agency, you may ask? Well, for one, a detective. As it was my idea, and I paid for everything, I, of course, filled that role. Next, I needed a secretary. My beautiful and marginally dangerous best friend Scarlett filled that role. Now, I will admit, at that time, I had not thought further than that, and simply skipped to getting my detective license, an office, and some other necessities.

My mind might have been too full of the fun adventures I was about to have. My hope was that those in and out of the paranormal communities would keep me entertained for a very long time. I quickly realized I still needed a driver, a tech person, and a witch that was good with ghosts. This is the story of how I found those people. And who would have thought the first to walk through the door would be human, with no knowledge of the paranormal—my precious Turney.

Author Note

This is a slow burn M/M paranormal romance book. It contains graphic language and adult sexual content. There will be blood, violence, and death. Please do not read if you find any of the previous triggering.

Dedication

Dedicated to all my friends who have encouraged me to write what I want and push past the self-doubts.

Prologue

Almost Ready?

"License, check! Office..." Octavius Evander spun around in his spinney chair. The practically empty office and his secretary—slash—friend's face blurring as he did so. Octavius had to admit it wasn't much of an office at the moment.

The building he had purchased was located in the busy side of the city of South Windsall, Connecticut, where many other businesses thrived. Did he need the whole four-story building? No, not really.

But Octavius had no intention of using all of it, or any plans to remove the current businesses working inside. His only interest had been a small office space on the third floor. Why rent one space when you can buy the whole building? Besides, now he didn't have to worry about gaining permission to make changes, or about getting noise complaints from nosy neighbors.

The office in question was rectangular, with white laminate floors and white walls. It was only about 1000 square feet and had a completely open floor plan. Practically empty except for a few bits of furniture left by the previous tenants. Bonus, the large window on the far side gave a gorgeous view of the ocean. It would do until they had time to renovate!

Octavius stopped spinning to finally say, "CHECK! Now..." He tapped his chin, thinking. "I just need a flyer! And maybe an accountant. Though, I suppose I can use my current one. We may need some cameras and a few candles, some decorations, a sign, a witch, a car—"

His eye twitched, as the last time he drove flashed to the forefront of his mind—the smell of burning metal wafted forward, as did the charred flesh and feeling of broken bones. Shuddering, he gasped. "No! No car, a driver. Okay, I need a lot more, but it's a start! But first off, a flyer!"

Octavius grabbed a blank piece of black paper from the rather large stack on his desk, before he pulled a pair of glasses out of his pocket and put them on—for aesthetic purposes only—and started to write and draw on it with a white colored pencil. Octavius worked on it for the next few minutes, scratching his brow every so often, before exclaiming in excitement that he had finished!

"How does this sound?" He cleared his throat and began to read out loud.

The Undead Detective Agency

LOST SOMETHING? *Relative dead and never told his secrets? Think your spouse is cheating or maybe a werewolf?! Got a 100-year-old murder to solve?!*

The Undead Detective Agency is here to help. We will

find, summon, and uncover all you need to know, before you even know you need to know it.

Call: XXX-338-8267
Currently hiring: a decorator (temp), a driver, a tech person (must be good with cameras and computers), and a witch (good with ghosts). PAYS WELL!

"HOW DOES THAT SOUND?" he asked Scarlett again, after she remained silent. His friend was giving him a rather incredulous look, he thought.

"Like you are a nutcase," the redhead mused dryly.

His smile fell. "But I think it's eye-catching! Don't you? I made a tombstone design and everything, look!" Octavius held it up to show her.

"Last time I checked, humans still outnumbered us paranormal creatures. Who are you planning to draw in with this?"

"Everyone!" he said, spinning in his chair again.

"Why is the paper black?"

Octavius really didn't want to answer that. "Just for fun."

"Okay, but why are the four boxes of paper in the corner marked 'office paper,' the paper I asked you to get, also all black?"

He scrunched down under her judging gaze. "Well, you see, we are The Undead Detective Agency. And I thought, well, why not stick with the spooky theme and only use black paper!? So, I bought it instead of white. I did then realize the issues we would have reading what we printed. So, I, being the smart person that I am, canceled our printer orders, and instead bought a few modified printers that print on black paper in white ink!"

"You couldn't have just returned the paper?"

Octavius gasped. "But the theme!"

She let out a long-suffering sigh. "Should you not at least put the hiring info on a different flyer?"

"But that would be such a waste of paper! Think of the environment!" Or rather, he had just spent all that time and didn't want to spend even more time remaking not one but two flyers.

"As much of a waste as an ancient vampire suddenly deciding to open a Detective Agency, for no other reason besides that he is bored?" she deadpanned, not even blinking —not that she generally needed to blink.

"Well...you eat brains. What do you know?"

"I can also eat delicious sweets, unlike someone I know. What about it?"

He dramatically grasped at his chest, his mostly unbeating heart under his palm, and let out a high-pitched whine. "How could you?! And what is so wrong with trying to get a hobby?"

Octavius' despair at never being able to taste, to savor solid sweets again, hit him like...well, much like that truck had hit him the last time he had driven. He still had hot chocolate, but it wasn't the same!

Scarlett Beaufort, his best friend, and the gorgeous zombie who perpetually appeared fed up with his existence, walked over and patted his back almost robotically. "There. There," she said, voice as stiff as wood.

Chapter One

The Call Of Fate

Scarlett watched, unimpressed, as Octavius attempted to command the phone to ring. The male was at his desk, hand hovering over the phone saying "I command you to ring"—it, of course, was not working. Vampires may have mind-control powers over a select number of creatures, but not over inanimate objects.

Her friend's hands dropped, and he slumped over in his old brown leather chair with a pout and began to spin in it—for the hundredth time. She had to say their current furniture and office supplies were lacking. The only supplies they had brought in so far were boxes of black paper—she scoffed internally at that—two specialty printers, and a red cradle phone.

Octavius abruptly stopped spinning, staring directly at her. "I don't understand. It's been two days already, but not a single call!"

Now Scarlett had some inkling as to why no one would call, but the vampire would likely become upset if she said why. Generally, she did not like making Octavius upset... unless she was in the mood to do so. For instance, when she felt like being entertained and not paying for said entertainment.

Why pay for a movie when Scarlett had a best friend who could be equally as entertaining? This was not one of those times, for making Octavius upset also meant having to comfort him, and she had to be in the mood for that as well, and frankly, she was not.

So she held back telling him the real reason. Which was, who would ever consider calling after looking at their hand-drawn flyer, with a description that sounded as if it was written by someone who had gone entirely around the bend?

Instead, she suggested, "Maybe we didn't print enough, or put them in the right place? Setting up a website, putting the ad online, or possibly in the paper, would probably help. Flyers are all well and good, but won't reach clientele out of the city. By the way, where did you have Henry put the flyers?"

Octavius looked at her with big glowing eyes and said, "Everywhere." He emphasized by waving his hands.

Her stomach dropped at his enthusiasm. A sneaking suspicion began to sink in, but she asked for clarification anyway. "Okay, but where specifically did you tell your butler to post them?"

Octavius' expression turned sheepish, his gaze sliding to the left away from her. And he said, way less dramatically this time, "Everywhere."

She sighed, her suspicions confirmed. Scarlett sat on top of her desk, arms crossed. "You didn't give Henry a single specific location, did you?"

Octavius peered back guiltily, hands twisting together on his desk. "Well, I wanted to be sure we didn't miss anywhere, so I thought..." He didn't continue.

"So, you thought?" She glared, her eyes filled with the judgment of all her many years of life.

"Everywhere would...cover..." Under her sharp, narrowed gaze, Scarlett's friend's voice became softer and softer until the words were inaudible.

She took in a deep gulp of air in preparation to scold him, when beyond all logic, the phone on Octavius' desk began to ring. Octavius freaked out at the sudden sound, toppled his chair, and disappeared behind his desk. The vampire shot back up to his feet, frantically reaching for the phone and knocked right into it, sending it flying off the desk.

Scarlett rolled her eyes at all this and caught the phone as it flew past her, calmly picking up the red receiver and answering it for him. One thing was for sure, she'd be damned if they'd wait in this office for calls—especially since nothing was set up yet. After this call, she would set up a forward, so all calls would go directly to Octavius' cellphone.

TURNEY PIMMS SCROLLED through his bank statements on his phone, with an ever-sinking feeling in his stomach.

Money was a funny thing. The cause of greed, desperation, of horrible human acts that many loved to cry were one-offs by some psychopath. But the truth was, most people were capable of doing awful things for money, for simply the reason that money made the world go round. Without it, you had and could do nothing.

Thus, Turney was placed in his current predicament. He either needed to find a job, or go back to his very illegal but not necessarily harmful ways—if you asked him.

On the one hand, if he did find a legitimate job, it would have to pay enough to cover his expenses—college, food, etc—which honestly was hard to find with a part-time job.

On the other hand, if he went back to his old ways—something he swore to never do—Turney could make enough money in a few nights to cover his expenses, and then some, for at least a year.

Then again, it would be hypocritical of him to be entirely against it. He had been living for the past seven years on said money, gotten through said illegal means. Until now, that is, since the money would dry up by the end of the month.

Illegal street racing would probably not look good on a lawyer's resume, nor would an arrest record. The main reason he stopped three years ago.

It was unfortunate Law School cost so much—or rather, Yale costs so much. He had saved money by finding a questionably cheap, but nice, house to co-rent. But it did nothing to cut the costs of the classes. And since he had " inherited" such a large sum, there had been no option of financial aid—he supposed he'd qualify now, hah.

Turney was honestly lucky to have gotten away with turning said money into a legitimate taxable source—thank you, adopted Great Aunt Trudy, may you rest in peace!

He flopped back on his bed with a groan.

Turney supposed...he could sell his car. Oh, but it was his baby, and it purred like heaven. How could he?! And really, a semester would pretty much eat up that money in a single go. Curse past Turney for not working the last few years to extend the money!

His roommate, Alexander Banks, burst into his bedroom without a single knock like always. The door slammed against the wall, causing one of his many stuffed animals to topple off the dresser.

Turney struggled to hold back his glare. Alexander was his landlord, friend, and roommate...and a bit of a pain in the ass at times. Not to mention, an eyesore in his overly bright clothing. The man's current outfit monstrosity was a t-shirt in an ugly fluorescent green with giant highlighter purple flowers. His bell bottoms would have been normal enough, if they were not in the same purple highlighter color. He was shoeless, but Turney knew the man had a pair of flip-flops the exact color green of the shirt. Man loved to match.

Anyone who saw him would think, maybe this was a costume? But no, this was just Alexander. His clothes were always a mixture of hippie and a bad acid trip; a lot of bell bottoms, and oversized clothing.

Clothing aside, Alexander was a handsome guy at six feet tall, with his natural golden bronzed skin, closely trimmed mustache and beard, and shiny curly shoulder-length black hair. Many would die for his high cheekbones, topaz eyes, strong square jaw, and straight hawk-like nose. If it wasn't for his clothes, the man could be mistaken for an actor or a model.

"Dude, look at this wacky flyer!" Alexander said with a laugh.

A black piece of paper was shoved in Turney's face. He rolled his eyes and took it from the man, preferring not to get a papercut to his eye. Looking at it, Turney would admit it was a bit wacky. Completely black, it appeared to be a copy of a hand-drawn advertisement for a Detective Agency.

With little emotion, he muttered out loud, "The Undead Detective Agency."

Was this a serious advertisement or a joke? For one, all the information was placed inside a hand-drawn tombstone, and the agency's name was underlined with what looked like vampire fangs. He scanned through it, more than ever thinking it was a joke with each word, until he reached the second to last line.

"Hiring a decorator, a driver…"

A driver! They were looking for a driver. Is this fate? It must be, right!? Why else would it have landed in his hands right as he needed a job? And driving, pft, no problem. He could handle that! Turney was an expert!

He looked up and found his roommate shifting back and forth on his feet, eyes shining with dumb excitement, waiting for him to react. Turney gave him a weak smile and tried to sound bored. "Sounds interesting."

"Right!?" The man continued to stare, with a giant smile on his face.

Turney often found Alexander's overwhelming sense of happiness creepy. He cleared his throat. "Anyway, I'm going to go use the restroom now." He slid out of bed and sprinted into his bathroom, with the flyer and his phone still in hand, slamming the door behind him.

Trusting this twist of fate, he dialed the number listed.

Chapter Two

Interview With A Human

Standing in front of his desk, Octavius nervously adjusted his tie. "How do I look?" He eyed Scarlett, who was sitting on the edge of the desk across from his.

His friend was as beautiful as always, with her large green eyes, pert upturned nose, and soft dimple on her chin. She had a classic red lip on. Scarlett's skin was perhaps a bit unnaturally pale, due to her zombie condition. This decade, she had decided to wear her bright copper hair at bob length, perfectly styled in waves and parted to the left.

Scarlett had on a dark green pencil skirt that had buttons down the left side. The skirt was paired with a tucked in, puffy-sleeved knit sweater in beige. It may be summer, but she was undead—overheating was just not a thing for her, or either of them, really. They could register the cold and heat, but it didn't negatively affect them.

Scarlett's eyes traveled over him. "You look as deceivingly put together as always."

"What's that supposed to mean?" Octavius glared.

She smiled brightly, but it didn't reach her eyes in the least. "Nothing at all."

Octavius huffed and messed with his tie again. "Your designer friend is coming tomorrow, isn't she?"

"Yes. At 8pm, as you requested, 'to set the mood,'" Scarlett drawled, making air quotes for that last part.

Her words sounded a bit disgusted to Octavius' ears, but he was so used to the tone he decided to just ignore it this time. "Good, good!"

"Did you do a background check on our interviewee today?" Scarlett asked, sounding bored, as she began to look at something on her cellphone.

What an odd thing to ask, he thought. "No?" he replied, confused.

She glanced up and gave him a look that suggested he had done something wrong.

"What?" Octavius asked, baffled.

"You're a detective, and you didn't even bother to check the background of a possible employee?"

"Well, I'll be able to tell if he's lying anyway."

"That's not the point!" Scarlett snapped.

Octavius wasn't really sure what her point was. He went to tell her so, but was distracted by a knock on the office door.

"He's here!" Octavius whisper-yelled, and clapped his hands together softly in excitement. He had heard the steps, the heartbeat approaching, but hadn't known if this person would pass by, looking for another office.

Octavius took a deep breath, gasping at the deliciously sweet scent that invaded his senses.

"He's HUMAN!" he whisper-yelled, in panic this time.

She shrugged and slipped off her desk. Her heels clicked on the hard floor as she made her way over to the door. "This is why you should have done a background check. Did you even look at the resume the young man sent in?" Her hand paused on the doorknob, and she glanced back at him with an accusing glare.

"I did!" He reached back and grabbed the clipboard on his desk, and held it up to show her. "Also, it's not like a background check, or his resume, would tell me if he is human or not. Most paranormals fake those anyway!"

Scarlett's gaze narrowed on the clipboard. "You looked at his face and stopped there, didn't you?"

"I did not!"

Okay, maybe he had. Frowning, Octavius walked around his desk, sat down, slipped on his glasses, and flipped the clipboard to face him.

The name on it read Turney Pimms, age twenty-five. The picture attached showed a young man with short, thick brown hair and sun-kissed skin. Oval face, aquiline nose, square hairless jaw, hazel green eyes, and nice lips. Turney was attractive. Not the most attractive man he had ever seen, but...who wouldn't want a handsome driver?

Octavius heard the door open and a conversation taking place, but tuned it out and instead actually read through the resume. It was a bit sparse. Only a single page, which mainly listed schooling, and the few months the man worked at some random fast-food joint. There was a large gap in his employment.

He didn't bother looking up until the human's scent grew close enough to taste. Which, with how sweet the human's natural scent was, he had a really strong urge to take a bite.

Octavius, at that time, stood up, gave a brilliant toothy smile, and held out his hand across his desk. "You must be

Turney Pimms? I'm Octavius Evander, the owner and lead detective of The Undead Detective Agency."

The man looked better in person—photographs rarely ever did anyone justice. Though...his clothes could be a bit more fitting. He supposed that the white dress shirt, black tie, and khaki slacks didn't look horrible.

The human's eyes widened in shock for just a moment before Turney returned the smile and muttered, "Hello," before grasping Octavius' hand and shaking firmly. He decided to not question the look and pushed himself to just smile brighter.

"Now then, why don't you sit down and tell me a bit about why you applied for the job." He waved his hand at the empty chair.

Human or not, Octavius needed a driver, and he was not about to discriminate based on species. Was it species... Was he a different species now? Octavius had once been human. A thought to ponder later, he supposed.

Also, it wasn't as if he had options at the moment. Mr. Pimms was the only one who had applied.

"Well, I have always been a strong driver," Turney assured him.

Hmm—truth. The man's voice was also pleasant to the ears. A deep timber that wasn't likely to get annoying—that was a plus.

"I noticed you have a rather large gap in employment. Can you tell me a bit about that?" Octavius asked, pretending like he had an actual interest in knowing.

He didn't particularly care about the reason. Octavius personally had a gap of about...he frowned—had it really been 300 years since his last official job? Either way, these were the sort of questions one asked during an interview.

Hehe—Octavius felt like he was role-playing how a proper boss conducted an interview. He grinned to himself and snuck a peek at Scarlett to see if she was proud of his professionalism.

Octavius managed to catch her notice, and to his shock, she rolled her eyes and shooed him with her hand—how rude. He sighed inwardly. Whatever, she would not stop his enjoyment!

"Um…"

At the utterance, Octavius' focus snapped back to the human who made the noise. Turney gave him a waned smile.

Ah—the man must have been speaking, and he had accidentally not heard—oops.

Octavius rubbed the back of his neck and apologized. "Sorry, could you repeat that? My mind wandered. My apologies again."

"Ah." Turney cleared his throat. "Yes, about the large gap in employment. I inherited a bit of money, so I didn't have to work for a while. But, I used most of it for my undergrad degree in Psychology, and then the rest has gone to pay for the past two years I've spent in law school."

Half-truth—the lie took place around the first mention of money. Octavius now had to decide if he cared. Maybe this could be a mystery he solves? Oh, how fun!

Forcing himself to focus and not let his mind wander again, Octavius asked, "Law school? What school are you attending?"

"Yale."

Octavius was impressed, but then again, those with money always tended to find a way into those types of schools. The ways of the world were the same no matter what century it was.

"Impressive." Octavius gave a fake smile. "So, tell me, Mr. Pimms. Why should I hire you to be my driver?"

"Well, I am experienced, as in I've had my license for years. No accidents on my record. And if there is ever a time we need to chase someone, I can guarantee that I will not lose the person, and that you will get to your destination safely and in one piece."

As someone with five explosive accidents on his record, his excitement built with each consecutive word after "no accidents." His heart had even given a few loud beats—and for him, that was rare.

"How fast?" He may have started bouncing in his seat —maybe.

Turney smirked, which just added to his good looks. "As fast as the car will let me."

Clapping his hands in excitement, a happy squeal burst out of Octavius. "You're hired! When can you start?"

Scarlett cleared her throat loudly. "Octavius, you skipped too many steps."

Octavius frowned...steps... And then it hit him what she was talking about. Oh—yes! He went to speak, but Turney beat him to it.

"Ah, yes. There is the matter of pay. The main reason I'm looking for a job is because the money I inherited is running out, due to the costs of school and living," Turney admitted hesitantly.

Octavius waved the issue away with his hand. Money was of no concern to him. The bulk of his estate kept gaining, and it was doubtful he'd ever be able to spend it all even in a hundred lifetimes. "How is $35 an hour?"

Turney choked and started to cough.

Octavius frowned at the reaction. "If it's too low, I could

go to $45 and maybe look into health care benefits." Not that Octavius had any use for healthcare himself, but he had heard it was a sore issue for humans—at least in the States.

TURNEY PINCHED his thigh in a way no one would notice. There was a sharp sting, but the scene in front of him did not change.

This was too good to be true. There had to be a catch. No way this position hadn't been filled yet. First off, the pay. Secondly, Octavius looked like a God, and had the voice of a wet dream. Turney had been so startled by Octavius' looks that he had even frozen at the sight of him.

A Greco-Roman statue is what the man reminded him of. Strong but not quite square jaw, with a rounded chin and high cheekbones. He had the classic Greek nose, plush lips, and glowing olive skin. On top of all those gorgeous features, Octavius had light, ocean blue eyes and short, curly, sandy blond hair. Perched on his nose was a small pair of oval rimless glasses, with gold accents that went perfectly with the rest of his outfit. And what an outfit.

Dressed to the nines in what appeared to be a well-fitted, tweed, gray-striped, buttoned vest and suit pants, with a beige, long sleeve, collared shirt with small purple stripes and a dark purple tie. The outfit was finished with dark brown laced boots. It all looked very expensive, and a bit heavy for summer.

Said gorgeous man looked to seriously be debating if his

offer was enough—did Octavius not even know what minimum wage was?

His soon-to-be boss—hopefully—waved his hand and said, "No matter. We can discuss pay and benefits a bit later. I'll have a contract drawn up, and we can negotiate. There are a few things we need to discuss first."

Turney had a feeling he was about to find out why this guy was willing to pay so much.

"Ah, yes. Later is fine. So, what is left to discuss? Though, I suppose I never mentioned that while I plan to go down to part time, I will need to work around my classes. I'm on break now, but a new semester will start in a few months. I hope that is fine."

"That shouldn't be a problem. I can just have my butler drive me when you aren't unavailable."

Butler? So, the guy was rich and maybe had no concept of money—that worked for Turney.

"All that aside, you have the job if you want it, as long as you can handle what I am."

"I want the job. No question about it," Turney stated without hesitation. Octavius could be in a cult, and Turney wouldn't have cared. He needed the money, and this was too good to pass up.

"Don't be so hasty, young man," drawled the woman, who had introduced herself as Scarlett.

Like Octavius, she was also too gorgeous to be real. Though, he'd have sworn she wasn't much older than him.

"Right, so I am a vampire," Octavius stated calmly, without even a hint of humor.

Yep, the other shoe had dropped. Okay, so Turney's future boss was crazy. This was not a deal-breaker. He could work with this. *Think of the money, Turney*, he told himself.

How did Octavius being crazy not make him less hot? "A vampire?" Turney rasped.

"Yes."

He forced a smile on his face. "Well, I mean, we all have our burdens. Right? No big deal."

Octavius' eyes seem to become unbelievably big and shiny. Turney had never seen a man appear so touched. And in the blink of an eye, he found Octavius in front of the desk, grasping hold of his hand.

How...had he gotten there so fast? Maybe Turney was the one losing it.

"Yes!" Octavius gasped. "We all do, don't we! Perfect! When can you start?"

Scarlett scoffed loudly. "He doesn't believe you."

Octavius' face fell. His hands released his, and he looked so sad—to the point Turney really wished that she had kept quiet. Turney had a thing for cute people, pets, and stuffed animals—Octavius looked awfully cute while pouting.

"I—" Turney went to deny it, but Octavius sighed, stopping him.

"Right, humans always need proof."

The man opened his mouth, and his teeth looked very white and normal, besides the tip of his canines looking a bit sharp. Turney's brows rose when they descended. He had to be honest; Octavius had some grade-A quality prop fangs. Many would pay good money for ones that dropped so smoothly.

Turney nodded. "Neat."

Octavius muttered something under his breath that, based on the man's expression, Turney would say was him cursing. Though, he wasn't sure in what language.

"Hollywood." Octavius huffed loudly and sat back on the edge of the desk. "Fine, how about this?"

Turney's eyes grew wider and wider as Octavius' form grew smaller and smaller.

"Believe me now?"

The voice was high-pitched, *very fitting for a bat* was his first thought in the blank slate his mind had turned into.

Chapter Three

Tell Me Everything!

Turney broke free of his shock, only to jerk out of his seat on instinct, heart racing in fear as fight or flight took over. He, of course, tripped over the chair and fell on his ass.

Ass throbbing from the fall, he froze where he sat, staring at the small bat. The bat was staring back at him with wide eyes. Turney was sure his eyes were just as wide when the bat morphed back into Octavius.

His initial thought that Octavius was crazy had now switched into thinking Turney was the one losing his mind.

Fangs were one thing. Turning into a cute, tiny bat was not exactly something he could logic away as an expensive prop. Especially as Turney had witnessed the multiple, freakishly formed, in-between stages as Octavius had gone to bat and back again.

"Wake up!" Turney squeaked, slapping his own face.

A loud feminine scoff came from behind him. Octavius seemed to be taking his actions patiently. A simple lifting of an eyebrow was the only clue to suggest the vampire found anything odd.

Turney's cheek stung, and the scene remained unwavering. This was most definitely not a dream. Though his throbbing ass, due to his fall, really should have told him that already.

Holy. Fuck. Vampires were real! This changed everything!

Turney frowned. And yet, nothing at all. But, in what capacity were they real? Were they cursed? Some freaks of nature? Were they a different species?!

Octavius remained leaning against the desk, waiting, expression hopeful—unless the small smile the vampire was giving him was more of a hungry smile…

Eyes narrowed, Turney asked, "Are you planning to suck me dry and throw my body in a ditch somewhere?"

Octavius chuckled. "No."

"Am I a backup food supply?"

"No." The male straightened, and still smiling, offered him a hand up.

Turney eyed the hand, and then the vampire's smiling face, and then the hand again. Clearing his throat, he accepted it, curious to see how warm it was. He couldn't remember from the earlier handshake if it had been cold or not.

The hand that met his was surprisingly warm, probably warmer than his own—bad circulation and all that. The grasp on his hand tightened, and he was yanked up abruptly. The momentum had him in the vampire's arms, flush against him, one hand pressed to Octavius' chest. And a very solid chest it was.

They were about the same height, he found, with Octavius probably having about an inch on Turney's six-feet. Heat spreading across his face, Turney stepped back. The vampire released him instantly. Turney stood there quietly for a moment, staring at the smiling vampire before awkwardly righting his chair and sitting down, as if he had not just freaked out—or groped his potential boss.

Octavius sat on the edge of the desk in front of Turney, his expression only becoming brighter.

"So," Turney murmured.

"So?" Octavius encouraged.

"Just to be clear. You're not going to eat me, and this is really just a job for a driver. But vampires are real, and you are one."

Though—his eyes swept over the vampire in question—maybe being Octavius' meal wouldn't be so bad.

"Correct. I do understand this may be hard to accept."

"A bit hard to digest, not necessarily accept." Turney nervously pulled on his tie. "Can I ask a few questions about the whole vampire thing? I mean, it's not every day you find out vampires exist."

Octavius pursed his lips, making Turney fear that all the questions running through his mind would remain unanswered. The fear was for nothing as the male's smile quickly returned, and he nodded. So, Turney didn't hold back.

"Is your vampirism science or cursed based?"

Octavius hummed. "More the latter. While new vampires can be born now, they started off as the result of two Gods fighting, rather than a simple curse from the heavens."

"That opened up more questions than answers. But I'll stay focused on the topic at hand." Mainly as he didn't want to know if God or Gods existed. His mind had already been blown once today. He did not need to tackle more.

"Do you need human blood to survive, or does any blood work?"

"Vegan vampires do exist." Octavius gestured towards himself. "I am not one of them. But it is possible to survive on animal blood. If you want to call consuming liquids that taste putrid daily, surviving." The male's tone of voice had turned mocking by the end.

It didn't sound like surviving to him, but he didn't bother saying so and instead asked, "Does the blood have to come directly from the source?"

"Bagged blood works as well as fresh. It is also much more convenient."

Turney imagined it would be. He glanced at Octavius' clothes, and a thought occurred to him. "Where do your clothes go when you change into a bat?"

Octavius' mouth opened and then closed, and he frowned before admitting, "I don't actually know. It is convenient that they disappear and reappear. I have never been a fan of public nudity."

And wasn't that a shame, for Turney would have loved to see everything. Shaking that thought away, as it was inappropriate to think such things about his soon-to-be boss, he moved to his next question. "Can you change into other animals as well?"

"I can change into anything my body weight or smaller. Though, I suppose I could take the form of larger animals if I tried, but they would be small versions of them. It's a distribution of mass. I can't become bigger than my own mass. I'm not sure what happens to the mass left over when I become smaller."

"So, you could like become a tiny elephant?"

Octavius' head cocked as if thinking on it, and then he smiled and let out a ridiculously adorable giggle. "I suppose I could."

"Cute," Turney cooed, and then, to cover up the slip, quickly asked, "Do you mind if I ask about weaknesses? I promise I have no intention of harming you."

And he didn't. So Octavius was different. It didn't give him a right to try to kill him just because he wasn't human. Turney had faced enough homophobes back when he used to race, the last thing he'd do was try to hurt someone just because they were different than him.

"You aren't strong enough to kill me, so go ahead," the male answered, very matter of factly.

Here's hoping he never needed to defend himself from Octavius then.

"So, sunlight?" Turney asked.

"Love it."

"Stake through the heart?"

"A nuisance at best."

"Does your heart beat?"

"Very slowly, or not at all if I'm low on blood."

Huh—interesting. "I'll come back to that. What about if your head is chopped off?"

"Depends on how long it is detached."

That one was slightly shocking. "You regenerate?"

Octavius smiled at him, as if he was happy Turney figured it out on his own. "I do. Rather quickly, I might add. Though the speed depends on how much blood I have consumed. I suppose I may die if my head was separated from my body for a few days...or weeks. Truth be told, it's not something I've tested, so I don't know exactly how long."

Made sense. Turney wouldn't imagine many would try to test that out themselves, vampire or not. "How about fire?"

"I burn about as easy as you would. No more, no less. It is not likely to kill me, however. I should add that while I do feel pain, it is not the same as how you would. I can tolerate a lot more."

"Crosses and other religious paraphernalia?"

The vampire shrugged. "Does nothing."

"Do you have a reflection?"

"I do."

"Garlic?"

Octavius grimaced. "Well, it won't harm me, but I can't really eat it."

"You can't eat it?" Turney supposed he should have asked first if Octavius could eat anything. "Can you consume anything besides blood?"

Nodding enthusiastically, the vampire's smile returned as he said, "Yes."

"But not garlic?"

The smile fell again, and a pout took its place. His bottom lip popped out, and everything. "I can't consume anything solid," Octavius admitted, voice coming out tiny.

It appeared that solid food was a touchy subject. The vampire even looked a bit in despair about it. So Turney tried to move past it.

"So, you can consume things as long as they are liquid?"

Octavius perked up a bit and nodded.

A thought occurred to him, and without thinking it through, Turney blurted out, "Do you poop?"

After the words were out, he slapped his hand over his mouth—shocked he actually asked that. Scarlett made a choking sound. Octavius blinked at him a few times, looking startled before bursting into laughter.

"I'm so sorry! I didn't mean to ask that. It just came out."

"No worry. And the answer is no, I do not."

Turney gasped. "Fascinating."

"I'm glad you think so." Octavius giggled.

Turney shook his head, trying to focus on the matter at hand, which was about how a vampire could die. "We've gotten off-topic. So, if none of those methods work. How can you die?"

"Complete destruction of my brain."

"That's the only way? What about diseases or things along that line?"

"Yes, it is the only way. And I can neither catch nor give human illnesses."

"Interesting." Turney rubbed his chin. "Are you alive?"

"Let me do a bit of an overview to see if I can answer the rest of your coming questions on that subject. I was, in fact, human once. I was born in 613BC, during what I figure was mid-July in what is now referred to as Ancient Corinth. If you don't know where or when, the best signifier is that it was before the time of the Romans, but the area did eventually fall to become part of the empire."

He choked on air. Holy shit—cute vampire was ancient! "You are how old?"

"I believe about two thousand, six hundred and thirty-five."

No wonder the male reminded him of ancient Greco-Roman statues! Octavius was literally born during the time!

"Either way, I was changed against my will soon after my twenty-eighth year. No, I will not answer any questions about how turning works. To summarize, I am not necessarily alive, but I am also not dead. I'm stuck somewhere in between. I drink blood, and have to do so if I want to remain awake. I mainly stick to bagged blood, unless I have a lover."

OCTAVIUS WATCHED Turney's eyes drop down and back. Face flushing on the way back up, as if not believing he had just done that.

Cute—Octavius had forgotten how flustered humans became when introduced to the unknown... Though, some got more stabby than cute. He supposed, in this case, being flustered was more about getting caught staring at his groin than about what Octavius was.

"Yes, besides my digestive system, and an organ or two, the rest of me, including my reproduction system, is fully functional."

"Sorry." Turney whimpered, face beet-red—ah, look at all that blood.

"The apology is unnecessary. I am not easily offended."

Scarlett scoffed loudly.

Octavius side-eyed her. "I'm not," he whined defensively.

"You can be sensitive," she stated.

"Not about unimportant things."

"Debatable."

"Hmph!" Octavius turned back and saw Turney was

eyeing Scarlett with interest. But there was nothing sexual about the look.

Smirking, he said, "So, as I was saying, I'm not alive, but in between. By far, I am not the most interesting of the undead paranormal. Scarlett, as a zombie, is far more fascinating."

Turney seemed to be returning to his earlier shock, before snapping out of it and grabbing his hand, shouting, "I'll take the job! Good pay and a chance to learn about the paranormal. How could I pass up the opportunity?!"

"Fantastic!" Octavius gasped. Standing up, he slapped Turney gently on the back. "So glad to have you aboard, and yes, we will run across plenty of paranormals in our work!"

Turney faced Scarlett, hand extended. He was no doubt about to speak when she crossed her arms, her stance stiffening up as she began to glare fiercely. As in zombie fierce. Her eyes turned bloodshot, skin becoming paler by the second, veins deepening and popping forward.

Hand falling to his side, Turney took a step back.

"Scarlett." Octavius glared pointedly at her. She sighed and instantly returned to normal.

"Yes, I'm a zombie," Scarlett practically hissed out. "No, I don't eat human brains, nor do I need to. Animal brains and other substitutes work just fine. Yes, I eat other food as well. No, I will NOT answer any other questions."

"Right," Turney croaked before clearing his throat.

"Don't mind her. She is always grumpy. I can—"

Scarlett stomped her foot and RUDELY cut him off. "You will not, under any circumstances, answer questions about me or my kind, Octavius."

Octavius stuck his bottom lip out at her, pouting. Still, he could tell, based on the tone of her voice, that she was serious —as in, he would regret it if he didn't listen.

"Fine!" Octavius huffed.

"Um, now that is settled...how about a test drive?" Turney suggested.

"Oh! Yes, a test drive would be wonderful!"

Chapter Four

Test Drive To Our First Case

The walk to Turney's car was a quick elevator ride down to the underground parking lot. He was curious as to why Octavius had put on his suit jacket before leaving, and started to wonder if vampires could feel cold, or even overheat, for that matter. Octavius had also removed his glasses, making him wonder if they were real or not.

As Turney approached his baby, he announced, "Here it is!" He pointed proudly towards his 2019 Toyota Supra.

Turney turned to see how Octavius was reacting, and the man had little to no reaction. He frowned. Turney had honestly expected one. While one couldn't see the upgraded turbochargers, the suspension changes, etc., the exterior should have warranted some sort of oohing and ahhing.

The front of the vehicle was painted in shiny, sparkly pink, that faded in gradient to purple, and then finally to a bright cyan. Turney's car looked a bit like cotton candy, but with deeper colors. Turney liked sweets, and the colors pink and blue...and just cute things in general.

"It's...turbocharged..." Turney stated hesitantly. He

tugged on his tie nervously—the damn thing felt like it was choking him.

Octavius continued to stare blankly, but did ask, "So, it can go fast?"

Turney nodded his head and tried to push away the disappointment. It was hard to accept that so few around him had any real interest in cars. But since Octavius didn't drive, Turney supposed he shouldn't be surprised at his lack of interest in cars.

Turney headed towards the driver's side, but thought better of it and went to the passenger side instead. Grabbing the door handle, the car unlocked automatically due to the fob in his pocket, and he opened the door for Octavius.

"Thank you." The male smiled and slid in.

Turney quickly walked around and got into the front. Pressing the start button, the engine purred to life with a smooth rumble.

"Where to, boss?" he asked.

"Hmm," Octavius hummed. His face scrunched up in thought before saying, "How about we just drive around without a specific destination?"

"Works for me."

Turney carefully made his way out of the underground parking garage and onto the roads. He then made sure to follow all the traffic laws. It was a test drive; running a stop sign or speeding wouldn't be good.

They only got about five minutes away from the office when Octavius' phone rang.

Turney eyed Octavius, as a song by a very popular Korean band, BTS, played loudly from his side.

He guessed their fans really did come in all ages—even ancient. The song cut off abruptly when Octavius pulled out his phone from his pants pocket and answered it. The man had a purple folding smartphone, so he flipped it open to answer.

"You've reached The Undead Detective Agency. Octavius speaking, how may I help you?"

A client? Turney glanced over and, spotting an almost empty parking lot, pulled off and parked, just in case they had to head back to the office.

Relaxing in his seat, he watched Octavius as he waited. The vampire's expression turned from hopeful to increasingly excited, to the point the male was bouncing in his seat.

"Yes!" The vampire nodded. "Yes," he repeated before asking, "where would you like to meet?"

Their first case already, Turney was mildly excited. If he were to judge by Octavius' expression, the case must be a big one. Though he wasn't sure how much work he would be doing, considering he was just a driver.

"Yes, we will be there in thirty minutes. See you soon," Octavius replied, before hanging up and putting his phone away.

"Good news?" Turney inquired with a raised brow.

"We have our first case!" the vampire shouted exuberantly.

Turney chuckled at Octavius' excitement. "That's great. Where to?"

"Franklin Fairwood Park."

Okay, the location sounded just a tad bit shady, but he was sure there was a perfectly plausible explanation, right? It was in a good neighborhood, at least.

Turney kept his opinion to himself and wordlessly put the car in Drive, pulling out of the lot. True to Octavius' words, it took them about thirty minutes to reach the park. Their destination had brought them out of South Windsall, through part of Onwood, into the edge of Franklin.

Franklin Fairwood Park was located in a very fancy neighborhood, where some houses were vast distances apart, and some areas were even gated. It was a medium-sized park with swings, a jungle gym, a few slides, a couple of sandboxes, and various other equipment.

It also appeared utterly empty at first glance. Which was odd for the time of year. It was June, summer-time, and just now hitting noon. Was K-12 not out yet?

The shady feeling returned ten-fold as he turned into a very empty parking lot—empty except for a single pink bicycle. The feeling worsened as he spotted a little girl sitting on a bench, on the far side of the park, staring directly at them.

She can't be, is the only thought he had as he pulled into a spot and parked, turning off the engine. That hope was dashed by Octavius jumping out and heading right towards her, not waiting for him.

Squinting at the two of them, Turney watched as they shook hands and obviously began to talk. He sighed and got out, praying he did not end up in jail—he was way too pretty for jail.

Turney, approaching with much hesitation, came to stand beside Octavius.

The little girl, who couldn't have been more than twelve-years-old, briefly glanced his way before completely brushing off his presence and focusing back on Octavius.

He honestly didn't know if he should be offended by that. While Turney liked cute things…kids had never been included in his list. Except for babies—as long as he could give them back. While she was sort of cute, with her blonde pigtails and pink overalls, her unimpressed expression was out of place on a child and...irritating.

Octavius cleared his throat and introduced them. "Veronica, this is Turney Pimms, my driver. Turney, this is Veronica Talbet, our client. She was just telling me of her suspicions."

Part of him felt happy that Octavius had chosen to include him. The other part was screaming about the word 'suspicions.' Followed by a complete urge to meltdown.

Why the hell was Octavius not worried about the SUSPICIONS others would have if they saw them right at this very moment.

Two grown men meeting up with a little girl in the park. He supposed they may assume they were a gay couple...

"Right, as I was saying. I believe my neighbor, Leon Dietrich, is eating people."

"You think he's eating people?" Turney choked out, his voice slightly hysterical even to his own ears.

She eyed him again. The look was not friendly. "Yes," she said, voice clipped.

He turned to Octavius to see how the vampire was taking this, and was shocked to find the male looking completely enthralled.

Ah—so this was how his job would go. Them running around, believing crazy nonsense. Turney supposed as long as he got paid for it...and didn't get arrested, he had no reason not to do it.

"AND WHY DO YOU BELIEVE THAT?" Octavius asked with interest.

"Too many people have gone into his house and not returned. Also, most are not the type you would expect to go into a stock market broker's house. Like homeless people. And some of the ones I saw going inside have since come up as missing." She paused to side-eye Turney before adding, "He is not human."

Veronica seemed to hesitate to say precisely what Leon was in front of Turney. Not feeling up to explaining the whole, 'the human knows about paranormals' thing, Octavius let the vague statement stand.

Either way, he'd be able to tell what Leon was upon meeting him. Though, he could still narrow it down through a few questions.

"How many have gone missing?"

"We are new to the community, so I don't really know. But since I've been here, which is two months, maybe three dozen."

Octavius' brow's rose, taken aback by the number. It certainly narrowed down the options, but the number was extreme, even for what he was thinking of.

Either it was all Veronica's imagination, or they had a very, very hungry wendigo on their hands. Nonetheless, it was worth checking out. One paranormal acting out was one too many. However, if the numbers were accurate, they might be looking at a group of Old Country wendigos. It could fall back on all of them in the end.

"So, will you help me?" Veronica shifted impatiently from one foot to the other. "My parents won't listen to me. But I know I'm right."

"I will investigate. But first, let's talk price."

Veronica nodded and began to rummage around in the mini pink backpack she had with her. Out of the corner of his eye, Octavius caught sight of Turney's face.

The human looked weirdly upset. Mouth a firm line, arms crossed, gaze empty—what was wrong with him? Shouldn't he be happy that they had a case?

"I have twenty dollars, and seven mint, collector's edition BTS photocards. It's from their very first fan meeting, nine years ago. It is the most expensive thing I own."

At the mention of BTS, Octavius' gaze shot back to Veronica. A squeal of excitement escaped him before he could contain it, as he set his sight on the cards. He didn't have those ones!

"DEAL!" he shouted without a single thought—besides him needing to get his hands on the cards.

Turney let out a squawk next to him, but Octavius chose to ignore it. There were much more important things to focus on at the moment. Besides, humans were weird. Who knew why they did the things they did.

Octavius reached for the cards, pouting fiercely when she pulled them away.

"You can have the money and three cards now. The rest will come on completion of the investigation. I promise you will receive them no matter what the final results. I just want to know the truth."

"But BTS are seven! You can't split them up. It would be like splitting up a family!" Octavius protested. Together or apart, the fact would always remain that BTS was forever seven.

Veronica grinned a very toothy, evil grin and giggled. "I know, so you better hurry up so they can be reunited."

She handed the money over with three cards.

Octavius took them with a huff. "Fine! Results will be forthcoming by the end of the day!"

She nodded and rattled off a location that, from his memory, he thought was about fifteen minutes away.

"Let's go, Turney." Without watching to see if Turney followed, he spun on his heel, walking back towards the car.

On reaching, Octavius tugged on the door handle and found it locked. Frowning, he glanced around, looking for Turney and not finding him. It wasn't until he peered back, that he noticed that Turney remained standing where he'd left him. "What are you doing, Turney? Let's go!" Octavius called out, confused.

Turney jerked out of whatever trance he was in, shook his head, and sprinted over to the car.

At the sound of the lock disengaging, Octavius got in and put his seatbelt on. It had been the one thing that had kept him from losing his head during at least three of his accidents —safety first, buckle up indeed.

Weirdly, Turney got in and started to drive without saying a word.

Huh—Octavius would have thought he'd have questions —oh well. Octavius looked around the vehicle before opening the glove box and carefully sitting the three cards inside. Thankfully, they were all in hard plastic sleeves, so he wasn't too worried they'd get damaged. *I'll be back for you, my babies*, he thought, before closing it. Later, Octavius would stare at them and add them to his collection. For now, it was time to work.

Pulling out his phone from the pocket of his trousers, he flipped it open and scrolled through the numbers until he found his contact at the police department and hit call.

"Police Commissioner Javin speaking."

"Javin!"

"Octavius, is that you!? Did you get a new number?" The man's brogue was deep. No matter how many centuries it had been, the other vampire had never managed to get rid of his accent. Though, probably more shocking still, was the switch from piracy to working for the law. Though, he supposed many pirates had worked for the law of one country or another, back in the day.

"Mm, you know me. I tend to misplace it every now and then. But I've been well. So, do you remember how I was planning to open a detective agency? Well, I did it!"

"Congratulations!"

"Thank you. So, anyway, I have this case, and I was wondering if you could check the background of someone for me?"

"Sure, no problem. What is the name?"

"His name is Leon Dietrich."

"Got it. Give me a few minutes and I'll email you the information. I do have to hang up now, though. Meeting. I'll call you later. We can get drinks together."

"Sounds good. See you soon. And I'll keep my eye out for the email."

Octavius closed his phone and held it, waiting for the email to come.

"Are you really taking this seriously?" Turney questioned, speaking at last.

He glanced over and found Turney gawking at him. Which seemed a bit dangerous, considering the man was driving, but what did Octavius know?

"It's a case. Big or small, all clients should be treated with the utmost respect and sincerity." Octavius shrugged.

Hmm...while he could be wrong, as Octavius had never been good at judging human emotion—well, he used to be okay at it in the past. But, really, they were such dramatic creatures. Always screaming, yelling about demons, and grabbing pitchforks—all sorts of nonsense. Octavius blinked, realizing he'd lost his train of thought, or rather he had never finished it... What had he...

Right! Turney! He would swear the man sounded upset.

"Now, correct me if I'm wrong, but are you upset about something?"

"Octavius, don't you find it a bit odd for two adults to run around harassing some poor man based on the imagination of a twelve-year-old?"

He supposed that if people were doing so based on a child's imagination, he...might. Really, he'd have to be in such a situation to actually know. Since he was not, Octavius couldn't answer definitively.

"Why do you ask?"

"Because we are about to harass someone based only on a little girl's imagination!" Turney snapped, quite hysterically, in Octavius' opinion.

"Ah, I see where the misunderstanding has come about. You are mistaken. Her accusations are very serious and credible."

"We're being paid in BTS photocards! How serious can it be?!" Turney cried out, sounding exasperated.

Ah, so that was where the upset had come about—

money. Humans did get a bit funny when they were worried about money.

"Oh, no. Worry not. What I, or rather the agency, gets paid for a job won't affect your salary."

"That's...not the point!"

It wasn't? Octavius frowned—he had been sure...oh, well, he'd try harder next time. Phone dinging, he flipped it open and went to his email. Octavius quickly read through the information.

Name: Leon Dietrich, Age: 40—probably fake. He skimmed through the male's employment history. After reading a bit, it all started to sound like blah blah blah and nonsense to him—how boring.

Octavius slipped his phone back into his trouser pocket. He realized then that Turney must have been talking. The human had the look of someone who had been ignored. Face all scrunched up and glaring—just full of irritation. It surely hadn't been important, right?

"Anyway, so, here's our plan!" Octavius announced.

Chapter Five

The Bat Slide – Breaking In As A Vampire 101

This was crazy—completely insane. Yet, Turney kept walking up the long-ass driveway, towards the brownish-red front door that would begin his life of harassing possibly guilty people. Possibly, as in unlikely, as in minuscule, as in not actually possible. Which Turney realized didn't make sense.

The neighborhood he was in was frankly affluent. The houses had sprawling green lawns—at least the ones that he could see did. Most had large trees and shrubbery blocking the view and maintaining privacy. Each house was spaced out, a good distance from the next. Turney was honestly curious how the little girl had even seen anything suspicious.

The house he was approaching, while it did have a sprawling lawn, it also had the trimmed trees and shrubbery to block the view from the road and neighbors. The driveway was about a football field length's walk from the street to the brownish-red front door. The house itself appeared to be three floors, white brick with a gray roof and trim around the windows, looking how all fancy homes of this size looked—

old, expensive—not for him. The three-door detached garage was nice though...

Plastering a fake ass smile on his face, Turney pushed the doorbell. There was a faint generic ringing sound, followed by fast-paced footsteps.

The door opened, revealing a very average and non-threatening looking man. Brown hair, brown eyes, perhaps neutrally handsome, his features mixed well together, but none really stood out. It was the type of person who you may look twice at, but would probably forget later. In his polo and khakis, the man just screamed normal. Though, he supposed there were a lot of normal-looking serial killers. If he had to place the man's age, Turney would say that he looked about his own—twenty-five.

"Can I help you?" Mr. Dietrich asked with a raised brow.

"Hi, yeah, sorry to bother you, but my car seems to have broken down." As any car would when you undid some spark plugs, Turney thought with an inner eye roll.

"Ah, and you need to call a tow? Phone died?"

"Ah, yes. Ah, I mean no," Turney fumbled with his lie. "I mean, yes. My phone died, but more I was hoping maybe you knew something about cars and could take a look at it? I know it sounds like an insane thing to expect from a stranger."

Because it was a completely insane thing to expect, and entirely Octavius' crazy idea.

Turney cleared his throat and added. "I'm short on money at the moment and a tow..."

"Ah, I see." The man's expression was slightly drawn, baffled even, but to Turney's shock, Mr. Dietrich said, "I actually do know a bit about cars."

Turney's brow rose at that.

THE MOMENT LEON was far enough down the drive, Octavius let out an evil giggle and started to hum, "Da, Da, Da."

He swooped down from the tree he'd been perched in, onto the ledge of what must have been a basement window sill. Octavius plastered his little bat face to the window. While taking a deep breath, he peered in. The male was definitely a wendigo. Leon had the crisp forest wind smell that all wendigos carried. Though, curiously, there was no underlying meat smell.

Hmm—the basement was a bit of a disorganized mess. There were well over ten tall stacks of boxes, some haphazardly on top of each other to the left and center of the room. To the right on the floor were plastic containers. Bookshelves lined the right wall. Nothing looked suspicious, but who knew what those boxes held.

Gently tugging on the window, he found it locked.

"Bat strength," Octavius squeaked out loud, with an excited giggle, as he latched his claws onto the bottom of the window and shoved it open. The lock gave some resistance but broke easily under his strength, producing a loud snap.

Octavius slid the window open just enough for him to slide in—which wasn't much as he was currently only about three inches in size.

Flattening himself onto his stomach, Octavius shimmied inside while saying to himself, "Shimmy, shimmy."

Once he had slid through, he peered around once again. Everything looked huge at this size, but the boxes specifically looked like an obstacle course waiting to be conquered. One stack of boxes was looking particularly perfect to land on—or rather, one level of the stack, despite having boxes on top, there was still enough room for him to land.

He jumped from the ledge, taking flight. It was dark, but Octavius didn't need to use echolocation, unlike regular bats. His night vision was as good as his day.

Octavius landed gracefully on top of the large box, but at the last moment, turned his simple landing into a rolled one for dramatic effect. In his rolling, he made it between two of the small boxes sitting on top.

Suppressing his giggle, Octavius army crawled between the boxes to the other side. Stopping short of the edge hiding him, Octavius peeked his head out. To the left and right were walls of cardboard, the box stacks taller than the one he was currently lying on. The only way forward was to the front and downwards—upwards as well, but where was the fun in that?

In front was a shorter stack of boxes. Down below looked to be an open box filled with foam packing peanuts.

Octavius launched himself out between the two boxes on a whim, and instead of soaring, he free-fell.

"Wheeeee!" he squeaked happily.

Octavius landed with an oof into the box full of packing peanuts. Squeaking happily, he rolled around and pretended to be swimming.

TURNEY LED Mr. Dietrich down the long driveway to his car. For some reason, having the guy behind him set his hair on end—like he was being stalked by a hungry animal.

The man whistled as they got close to his baby. "Interesting car you got there."

"Ah, yes, it is. It was my brother's. I—" Turney paused, pretending to be choked up for dramatic effect. After milking it a bit, he added, "I inherited it after he passed on."

Turney, of course, did not have a brother—or any siblings. But, if the guy knew anything about cars, he'd notice the modifications when they popped the hood. Best to cover his ass.

"I'm sorry for your loss."

"I would have sold it, but it's all I have left of him. He was the only relative I had left, so… It's hard to let go."

"Understandable," Mr. Dietrich murmured.

Reaching the hood of the car, Turney turned back and met the other man's eyes. Instead of the sympathy that should have been there, he could have sworn he saw a spark of interest. Maybe he imagined it? Or perhaps the guy was just thinking about his car?

Clearing his throat, Turney popped the hood.

"What an engine," the guy gasped. "I can tell it was tuned for speed. Your brother had skill."

Turney laughed, slightly pleased as it was not often he ran across someone who could match his passion for cars—at least, not since he had gotten out of street racing.

OCTAVIUS FLEW AROUND the hanging light fixtures, softly squeaking the theme songs from the spy movie he watched last night. He was pretending the lines of the lights were lasers.

Quickly growing bored, Octavius landed on top of the closest bookshelf to the right and looked around for something else he could play with. That thought came to a crashing stop.

Wait! He wasn't supposed to be playing around. He was supposed to be investigating—*think of the BTS cards,* Octavius told himself with a smile.

Yes, BTS! No—he frowned—the investigation, for he was a detective! Octavius hummed—though being a spy would have been cool.

Octavius shook his head and pushed the thought away. He had committed and made his choice—a detective he would be. Besides, Scarlett would have probably strangled him if he tried to change his mind now.

Clamping his clawed feet on the edge of the top of the bookcase, he flipped forward to hang upside down and glanced over the content on the top shelf.

"Hmph. Why would a stockbroker have so many books on human anatomy?"

He dropped down and walked forward. On briefly reading over the names, Octavius found that everything on the first shelf was the same topic. Latching on to the left edge of the bookshelf, he slid down. On realizing it was more on anatomy, Octavius slid past the second shelf. Reaching the third shelf, he swung himself over on a high-pitched "whee."

The third shelf was a bit of a mess. Books were placed horizontally, all different shapes and sizes packed in right to the top—it was complete chaos, and it bothered Octavius' sensibilities to an extent.

"*Cooking with Garlic: Just the meats,*" he read. It was the first title he saw. Octavius scanned the first stack and found that the rest were cooking books, and not surprisingly, all dealt with meat.

A wendigo's primary food source was meat, and lots of it. But this did not tell Octavius what kind of meat the male was eating.

He walked forward. Eyeing the next stack, and on seeing more mass-printed cookbooks, he went past it. Octavius stopped in front of the third stack, as something caught his eye.

Smack in the middle of the third pile was what looked to be an ancient blue book, with a thick spine covered in wear and tear, and a handwritten title in German.

"*Das Festmahl der Götter.*" Octavius read the title aloud before translating it, "Feast of the Gods."

It sounded pretty promising. Not wanting to cause too much noise, he clasped his claws on the luckily slightly protruding spine of the book and gently tried to slide it from the stack. "And, we takes," he said to no one while feeling cute.

Except the book did not budge. Using a little bit more force, Octavius tried again. "And, we takes," he repeated.

Once again, the book stayed put.

Octavius let out a high-pitched hiss in frustration. "And,

we takes!" he squeaked loudly, tugging on the book with as much force as he used to break the window lock.

The book came flying free and slipped out of his claws to fly across the room. It slammed into a pile of boxes, knocking them over and causing a few loud thuds.

This would normally have concerned Octavius if he would have had the time to even think about it. But as the bookcase jerked forward with the book, he had other things to worry about.

Octavius let out a loud screech, wings flailing as the bookcase toppled forward—all of its contents cascading down.

"WELL, here's your problem. A few of your spark plugs have come loose." Mr. Dietrich reached in, no doubt to reconnect them, when there was the sound of multiple things crashing, followed by a loud boom coming from the direction of the house.

Mr. Dietrich's expression turned suspicious. His gaze flicked to Turney.

Turney did his best to look confused, but in reality, his insides were churning in full-blown panic. "Wonder what that was," he mused, hoping he sounded convincing.

The man straightened from his hunch and, without a word, spun on his heels, walking back up the driveway.

"Um..." Turney followed behind, stopping short of

entering Mr. Dietrich's house. Not that he could, for the man slammed the door shut in his face.

"Shit!" he swore.

Octavius, what the hell did you do? He pulled out his phone in a panic, called the vampire's number, and got a "user out of service" message.

A thought occurred to him: Could Octavius even answer his phone in bat form? It no doubt disappeared with the rest of his clothes when he transformed.

"Shit," Turney swore again.

OCTAVIUS CRAWLED out from beneath the bookcase, coughing and sneezing from all the dust. Thankfully, all the books falling down, and the many containers and boxes had given him plenty of cracks to shove himself into. He'd been able to stay safe and crawl to freedom.

It was unfortunate that he did not have the benefit of vampire speed in bat form. He always wondered why certain traits carried over when he transformed, but others did not.

Octavius sneezed again and attempted to brush the dust away, but froze at the sound of a door slamming and footsteps above.

"Uh, oh..."

TURNEY SHIFTED ON HIS FEET, feeling awkward. He wasn't sure if he should go back to the car and wait, or stay there and creepily stand on the dude's porch... Or maybe he should try to break in and save Octavius?

Luckily, he did not have to decide. There was the sound of footsteps and panicked squeaking coming from inside, followed by the door being opened by a now furious Mr. Dietrich.

"Uh...hello, again."

Turney glanced down to see a tiny bat struggling to break free, squeaking up a storm.

"You have a pet bat?" Turney asked, trying his best to appear shocked, which wasn't that hard as he felt very shocked but for other reasons.

Mr. Dietrich scoffed and shoved tiny bat Octavius into his hands. "Nice try. Take your vampire and go. Human or paranormal, you are all alike. Always assuming the worst. I may be a wendigo, but I am an upstanding citizen of the community. Now, leave before I call the police!"

The door was slammed in his face once again.

Wait...the guy was a wendigo?! As in, a scary people-eating creature? "Holy fuck, he's a wendigo?!"

Turney glanced down at Octavius, expecting some sort of explanation, but found himself looking at the saddest, poutiest bat he'd ever seen. The bat's wings were drooping down, and his eyes filling with tears.

When Octavius did answer, it was in a soft, sulky squeak. "Yes."

Turney glanced at the door and then back down at Octavius, before he decided he didn't want to be this close to the wendigo's house any longer.

Jogging back to the car, he questioned, "Shouldn't we tell someone? Isn't he dangerous?"

"There is no evidence." Octavius hiccupped before continuing sadly. "No evidence he eats people. I didn't find anything. He must just eat animal meat."

Turney switched Octavius into one hand and leaned over the hood to reconnect the spark plugs, before shutting the hood as he processed what the vampire had said.

"There are good wendigo?"

"There are good and bad of all paranormal creatures. Well, most. There are, I suppose, a few who are inherently evil, but not many."

Even with that bit of information, Turney still didn't want to stay there any longer. He quickly got in the driver's seat and sat Octavius down in the nearest cupholder. Turning the car on, he took off.

"I failed," Octavius cried. "My first case was a failure. I was wrong!" The vampire let out a very high-pitched wail of despair.

Chapter Six

Ice Cream! Ice Cream! Chase?

Turney eyed the teary-eyed bat and had the strongest urge to pick him up, pat his head, and tell him everything would be alright. Which he would not be doing. Octavius was his boss—soon to be boss? Was Turney even being paid for today? Whatever, he'd figure it out later.

Either way, Octavius was over two-thousand-years-old. He doubted the vampire would want to be babied...

As Turney continued to eye said two-thousand-plus-year-old bat, he started to doubt that Octavius wouldn't want that. But it would still be weird to pick him up—Turney was also driving. Okay, he'd compromise. No to picking him up, but yes to trying to cheer him up.

His mind ran through the various eateries in the area before hesitatingly suggesting, "Why don't we get some ice cream?"

Staring at Octavius out the corner of his eye, he watched with amusement as the vampire morphed from sad bat to the embodiment of an excited child.

"Ice cream!?" Octavius asked in his cute, high-pitched

bat voice. "But I failed," he said with a pout, returning instantly to sulky, sad bat.

"Hey, it's our first case. And I wouldn't say it was a failure. So, Mr. Dietrich doesn't eat people. You can't be right all the time. Besides, you still investigated, didn't you? That was the job, wasn't it?"

Octavius' head cocked. "I...suppose... I did investigate." The bat blinked, and then his eyes widened a bit, his expression slowly brightened again. "I did investigate!" Octavius said confidently this time.

"Yes, you did!"

Octavius gripped the edge of the cupholder and started to bounce. "Ice cream! Let's get ice cream! Or rather, a melty milkshake!"

"A melty milkshake it is!"

IN HUMAN FORM AGAIN, Octavius jumped out of the car once it was in Park. Not holding back his squeal of happiness, he ran up to the cutest ice cream parlor he'd ever seen. The establishment's name was in neon lights on top of the roof above the door, and it read *Cot and Candy's* in teal, and smaller writing below read *Ice Cream* in pink.

The creamery was white with an awning-like roof striped in white and baby pink. The double doors were glass, trimmed with that color of teal that was common in the sixties. The large windows on each side of the door had the same trim, and you could see people eating inside.

The outside eating area had old fashioned diner chairs made of chrome, with baby pink cushion seats and tabletops.

The door jingled as he pushed it open. Octavius found that the inside was just as cute as the outside. The same coloring, except for the black and white checkered floors. The order counter was teal and white marble, with one side a glass display showing all the flavors of ice cream.

A worker stood near the cash register, in a blue and pink striped polo with a pink bowtie. She had medium-length blonde hair, pulled up into a ponytail and was quite pretty, but her looks were of no interest to him. What interested Octavius was what was behind her. There was a giant wooden framed board on the wall that listed all the ice cream, milkshakes, and a variety of other ice cream related products the shop had for sale. Surrounding the board in various sizes were dozens of wooden framed drawings of ice cream and other desserts.

While the tables and booths inside were occupied, Octavius wouldn't say the parlor was busy. There was no line, or even anyone at the front counter waiting to order. Of course, it was also 2pm on a Tuesday. He wasn't sure if 2pm on Tuesday was a popular time to eat ice cream?

Octavius approached the counter and looked up at the board filled with all types of frozen goodies. With a sad sigh, he glanced past the more solid varieties to focus on the list of milkshake flavors. The door jingled again, but he continued to read as the smell told him it was Turney. The man came to stand beside him, looking up at the board as well.

After going back and forth between peanut butter chunk and mint chocolate chip, Octavius forced himself to pick one.

"I've decided!" he announced, turning to Turney. "Are you ready to order?"

The man smiled and nodded.

With that, Octavius approached the counter. The worker smiled brightly at him and asked, "What can I get you?"

As he was not one to be outdone in perkiness, Octavius returned the smile tenfold and gave his order. "I would like a medium mint chocolate chip milkshake. But I would like it to be mixed to the point that the chocolate chips are a fine powder and for the milkshake to be mostly melted. The chocolate chips can be switched out for chocolate syrup if that makes it easier for you. Though, I imagine the chocolate chips are already in the mint ice cream. Either way, medium melted, very mixed, finely crushed, chocolate chip mint milkshake."

Her bright smile seemed to falter just a tad before returning to its earlier voltage. "I'll...see what I can do. Anything else?"

Octavius could tell she was hoping he said no. He held no ill will. Octavius knew his order was unusual, and possibly a pain to make. Her being human, she wasn't aware that he was doing it out of necessity.

If the chocolate chips were solid, they'd turn to ash in his mouth. Milkshake with bits of ash was not a good combination. Ash really didn't combine well with anything, to be honest.

"Not for me. You're up, Turney." Octavius hummed as he stepped to the side.

Turney moved closer to the counter and ordered. "I'll have two scoops of cotton candy in a bowl, please."

The worker looked instantly relieved that it was not

something complicated and asked, "Will that be all for you two?"

"Yes," Turney replied.

"That will be ten seventy-nine, and it may take a moment for the milkshake."

"No problem." Octavius waved away her concerns about having to wait. He pulled out his small leather wallet from his waistcoat pocket, removed his black credit card, and handed it over.

The worker rang them up and went off to make their order. Over the next fifteen minutes, there were a series of grinding noises and other machine sounds. But, soon enough, she returned with their dairy delights.

They took their goodies and some napkins to the car. It was too hot to sit outside—well, too hot for Turney. Octavius really wasn't affected by temperature change. His body maintained an average of 95 degrees, and rarely fluctuated from it. While he could tell if something was hot or cold to the touch, it didn't negatively affect him as it did humans. No overheating, sweating, or feeling chilled to the bone—well, not unless it was extreme temperatures, such as if he were on fire, or in the arctic or something.

Once seated in the car, Octavius took a deep drink of his melty mint smashed chocolate chip milkshake—and it was perfect!

"Mmm," he groaned around the straw. The mint and chocolate flavors spread deliciously over his taste buds.

Turney chuckled next to him. "That good?"

Straw still in his mouth, he nodded.

Turney smiled at him like he was looking at something precious—which he was, so it was a fitting smile to throw his way. Where else would one find a vampire as cute as himself?!

In Octavius' vast and non-biased opinion, he had done an excellent job picking his driver. And it was not JUST because he was a sweets addict, and Turney had suggested they get something sweet. Though, that was a factor. And Octavius was struggling to name any other reason besides that. But he would definitely try to do so later when he wasn't distracted by the sweets.

Sweets, both in his mouth and invading his nose. Turney's ice cream was so sweet that it made the human's naturally sweet scent even sweeter than normal. Which was another added factor in his distraction by sweets.

Peering out at the street as he drank, he blinked in surprise at the sight of Leon Dietrich driving along the road. His eyes narrowed as suspicion welled up inside him. And at that moment, something clicked into place, making him almost drop his milkshake.

"Woah," Turney exclaimed, hand now under Octavius' cup. "Careful there. Wouldn't want to waste it by spilling it all over my car."

"You smell sweet!" Octavius gasped.

"Uh...thank you?" Turney murmured awkwardly, brows pinched.

"You are eating super sweet ice cream, so now you smell sweet! I mean, you always smell sweet, but now you smell like pixie sticks sweet! Leon Dietrich just smelled clean!"

"And that tells us..."

"He's hiding something!" Octavius yelled excitedly. "Follow that blue car!"

He pointed frantically. Though it was unnecessary. The traffic on the road was at a standstill due to a red light.

Turney looked confused, but to his credit, he sat his ice cream in a cup holder and started the car. The human managed to pull out into a wide gap caused by a vehicle turning slowly into the ice cream parlor parking lot.

They made it onto the road just as the light turned green. Turney appeared to be trying to keep some distance between them and Leon. Octavius figured it was a good idea. It wouldn't be good to be spotted.

"So, you want to explain the whole smell thing?" Turney asked, eyes remaining forward on the traffic and the blue car.

"Often, we pick up the smell of the food we eat. It clings, especially directly after consuming it, or if it's something that is eaten in obsession. And I'm speaking on overall scent, not just someone's breath after eating. Most of the time, humans won't be able to notice unless it is something pungent, as it's usually a very subtle change. While you smell super sweet to me now, no human would notice a change."

"So, because Mr. Dietrich doesn't smell like anything, he must be hiding something? And since he wouldn't need to do that if he was surrounded by humans, it means he probably encounters other paranormal species regularly enough that they would pick up on his smell. He also wouldn't need to hide anything if he was eating what he should," Turney deducted.

Octavius smiled, happy at the fact Turney had caught on so quickly. "Exactly." He nodded and then explained, "Wendigos, as a species, must take in large quantities of meat to keep functioning. To put it into perspective, they need to eat twice their weight in meat each week. So, all wendigos should carry around a faint smell of animal meat or by-products. It would take a lot of effort to cleanse the smell away. And it would be pointless to do so, since it's not like he can stop eating. So—"

"—The only reason he'd bother doing it is if he was eating humans, right?" Turney finished the thought for him.

"Exactly!"

"What do you smell like?" Turney asked, sounding curious.

"Me? I would imagine, like most vampires, my scent is probably mixed with a bit of copper because of the blood I consume. Otherwise... I've been told I smell strongly of cinnamon and balsam," Octavius said before picking up his milkshake and taking another long sip.

"Out of context question. Can you not eat ice cream unless it's melted?"

"I can, but it's much messier and takes longer to consume. And if it's not melted enough, there is always the risk of it turning into ash in my mouth, which is a very unpleasant experience."

"Wait. So if something is solid, it turns to ash?" Turney asked, sounding shocked.

It appears he had blown the young human's mind once again. He just wished it wasn't because of his devastating inability to eat solid food. "Yes."

The conversation lulled, and the drive continued. They had left the more populated area of the city of Onwood, and were now nearing the Onwood factory district that was close to the docks. It had been thirty minutes, and the further they went, the fewer cars were on the road, and the greater the distance Turney put between them and Leon Dietrich. Octavius would assume it was to avoid getting spotted. It did then occur to him that Turney's vehicle was a bit flashy. And now that it occurred to him, he felt the need to point it out.

"Your car is a bit flashy," Octavius hedged.

"Yeah, I—SHIT!" Turney swore, whatever he was going to say lost, as he reacted to the blue car taking a sudden sharp turn to the right many feet up ahead.

Turney did something to the—well, Octavius wasn't sure what he did, but he pulled something—and told him to "hang on."

Hang on to what, was all Octavius had a chance to think before the car shot off faster than he had that one time he went off that unfinished bridge.

Chapter Seven

Follow My Nose

Turney chuckled at the yelp Octavius let out at him drifting around a corner. Going at least thirty over the speed limit, he easily caught up with the blue Subaru. Bumper to bumper now, the car took off, taking turns as sharp as his had been.

He grinned, feeling a rush of familiar adrenaline—Turney had never been one to turn down a challenge. Shifting gear again, he matched the car speed for speed, sharp turn for sharp turn.

Octavius' little yelps of fear soon turned to giggling, and him every so often yelling "whee," once the vampire realized they were not going to crash—it was endearing.

After chasing Mr. Dietrich for a while, Turney noticed they were being taken further from where he had assumed the man had been heading.

"This could be a horrible idea, but how about we let him get away?" Turney suggested. He was going too fast to risk glancing over at Octavius. But when there wasn't an instant rebuttal, he explained. "Before being spotted, I think Mr. Dietrich was headed towards the factory district. We are getting further from that, as he tries to get away. If we let him think he has successfully lost us, he may head back to where he intended to go."

"It's a risk as we don't know how easy he will be to find in that area, or if he was really going there," Octavius remarked.

"Before he veered off, the factory district and the docks were all that was in the direction he'd been going. Neither are very big or well monitored by police. The specific area is mostly abandoned factories and buildings. And the port is no longer in use, due to it being deemed unsafe and a habitat for some rare bird species. Though, on the downlow, I've heard it was really just an excuse to relocate it to benefit some rich businessman. Anyway, it's your decision, boss."

Silence reigned for a few moments, besides the rumble of the engine, before Octavius answered him.

"Let's do it. Besides, we can't keep driving around like this. It's bound to draw police presence sooner than later."

Nodding, Turney purposely took the next sharp turn slower than he had been. He kept it up, slowing more each time until he thought it was plausible for him to lose the man. Two car lengths apart now—when Turney took the next turn to the right, the blue car was nowhere in sight.

It was obvious that Mr. Dietrich had taken the side street to the immediate left on entering the road. The blue Subaru would have still been visible on what was a long stretch of road with no turn-offs otherwise. Turney, of course, sped past it and down the street—pretending to be looking for the other car.

"It's done," Turney announced, slowing down to regular traffic speed before pulling into a vacant lot. It was good that the chase had ended when it had. A few roads over, and they'd have reached a more populated area...with traffic cams.

"I'm guessing we are going to wait here for a bit?" Octavius asked.

Turney nodded. "He needs to think he's safe, or Mr. Dietrich won't risk going wherever he was going."

He turned to the vampire, whose expression seemed calm, even though the evil people eater was out of sight. Turney had to admit, he was feeling envious of Octavius' settled emotions, as his stomach was churning in worry at the thought.

"No doubt," Octavius agreed before meeting his gaze, eyes sparkling and seeming way too interested.

"Uh...yes?"

"Where did you learn to drive like that?"

Shit—Turney's mind began screaming to lie like crazy, but all that came out of his mouth was...utter nonsense.

"Um, you see. Well, I-that is my...and um. Yeah."

Octavius chuckled. "You really don't want to answer, do you?" The vampire smirked and added, "I feel now would be a good time to tell you that I can usually tell when someone lies to me."

Turney sputtered and felt his face become molten as he crammed his lips shut, which just caused Octavius to burst into a fit of giggles.

"I'm guessing it was nothing legal," Octavius stated with a grin that ran ear to ear. "Since you don't want to talk about it right now, I'll leave you be. However, when you are ready to talk, please let me know. I'm sure it is a fascinating story. And don't worry, I have no intention of getting you in trouble with the law."

"I'm—" He frowned. "Maybe later," Turney muttered weakly.

Maybe when he didn't feel like he was on the edge of a full-blown meltdown. A bit too much had happened today.

"Well, we should get going, should we not?" Octavius drawled with a smile.

TURNEY HAD FUCKED UP. What the hell had he been thinking? *Oh, let's lose him,* he mocked in his head—what a fucking stupid idea.

Well, they had certainly lost him. They'd driven throughout the various roads around the factory district, and the Onwood docks, and not a single blue Subaru in sight.

They were currently driving along the road closest to the water. Seagulls cried loudly above, waves splashed down, and the area was pretty much empty. The once busy port and wooden docks were abandoned and starting to fall apart. Octavius was staring out the window at the water.

Time to own up to his mistake. Clearing his throat, Turney pulled off to the side of the road, putting the car into Park. "I'm sorry," he blurted out, when Octavius glanced over in question.

The vampire's right brow rose. "For?"

Why did the look make him want to confess all his sins? Not that the male looked particularly mad or anything. It was just that his expression was so clueless that Turney felt guilty.

"For losing Mr. Dietrich. For my dumb idea of not chasing. For—"

Octavius held up his hand, motioning him to stop, so Turney snapped his mouth closed and shut up.

"Relax, Turney. Sure, so far, driving around has not yielded much result. But all is not lost. And your idea was not stupid. Chasing him was getting us nowhere."

"I know, but at least we would still have him in our sights."

"And what would we have done with him?" Octavius asked. "If the man had stopped running, what would have been accomplished?"

"We..." Turney's words faltered.

Well, not much, if he thought about it. It wasn't as if they had any physical proof at the moment. They weren't legally wrong for following him—if you ignored all the traffic laws he'd broken. But they'd been safe in that aspect, due to no road cams on those streets

"I can see the wheels turning, but no words are coming out," Octavius noted. "Nonetheless, I'm sure you understand. While we don't know exactly where he is, we are still in a better place than before."

"Yes," Turney conceded. "But, what do we do now?"

Octavius' head cocked, and he hummed before saying, "Now, you drive us back a bit closer to the factory district, and find a place to park where we won't get towed. Then we get out and search on foot."

"That's a lot of ground to cover."

"Not with my senses," Octavius assured him.

Turney sighed, put the car back in drive, and did a very illegal U-turn. Five minutes later, they parked in a lot hidden between two abandoned factories. It had a barely hanging on, rusty sign saying *Public Parking*. Turney prayed his car didn't get stripped.

They both got out. After locking the doors, Turney waited for Octavius to guide them with his 'senses.' He really hoped they worked as well as Octavius claimed they did, or else they'd be wandering around until nightfall.

Octavius closed his eyes and took a deep draw of air. It was honestly probably the first time he had seen him breathe. Did the vampire need air?

Turney jerked back, cursing when Octavius' eyes opened, and instead of the ocean blue he was used to, they were solid blood red pools—no pupils.

"Warn a guy will yah!" Turney grasped at his chest, trying to calm his pounding heart. "This poor human just found out about vampires today. Your heart may not need to beat, but I will die if mine stops!"

"Apologies, I forgot how sensitive humans were to such things." The tone of the male's voice was not in the least bit apologetic. More amused, if he were to call it anything.

Turney scoffed but said nothing.

Octavius took another deep breath and announced, "I smell blood."

"Not to doubt your vampire powers, but it's not my blood you are smelling, is it?" Turney hesitantly asked.

Octavius rolled his eyes at him—which was very creepy due to their red coloring, and the lack of pupils. "The blood is not on the inside of anyone. Follow."

A chill went up Turney's spine. Not on the inside—oh joy.

Octavius started off, guiding them through the maze-like back alleys, taking them towards the docks they had left just minutes ago. After many turns, they stopped at the edge of where the docks and the factory district met—right in front of an old, abandoned paper mill. A chain-link fence surrounded the building. The place appeared to be multiple levels; its large smoke tower blackened on top. It was obviously falling apart, with boarded-up windows and white paint peeling off the brick.

"Here...it is here," Octavius announced, staring up at the tall factory with his dark red eyes. The vampire's nose wrinkled in disgust. "I smell blood, both old and new...and decay."

Chapter Eight

Reapers

"So, what's the plan?" Turney prodded, disrupting Octavius' thoughts.

Well, not necessarily thoughts, more the intense trance the smell of this much blood had over him. Shaking his head, Octavius closed his eyes and pulled back from what he liked to call 'super vamp' mode. The mode heightened all his senses, and allowed him to experience more of the world around him. It also always led to a massive headache that lasted for hours, and one not even drinking blood could cure.

Octavius could feel a dull throbbing already, and couldn't help but sigh in relief as things returned to normal. However, the smell of blood was still pretty bad, even in normal mode. How many had this bastard killed?

"Um, Octavius?"

His gaze pulled away from the building. "Yes?" Then it hit him. "Oh, right! The plan."

"Yes, the plan."

"Right, so normally I would at this point call someone to report it."

"The police?"

Octavius burst into a fit of giggles at the ridiculous notion. The police? Really, what could they possibly do to help—come and get eaten? Ah, humans were funny creatures.

"No, you silly boy. Reapers. I would, and will, report to the reapers."

Turney took on the expression of a frightened animal.

Right...humans new to the paranormal world equaled frequent freakouts.

"Reapers are real too!?" Turney yelped, voice a few octaves higher than usual.

"Not so much in the sense of the Grim Reaper mythology. They do not harvest souls to take to the other side, or work for death, or whatever nonsense you all made up about them. They do have a scythe, so you humans should feel good about getting that right. But while their being in existence does involve humans, they are no threat to you."

Turney took a deep breath and seemed to calm down a bit. He was getting some of his color back. *That had to be a good sign,* Octavius thought.

"So, what exactly are they, and what do they do?"

Octavius hummed, tapping his chin. "Well, to explain succinctly, they are immortal creatures who were created by a specific God to punish paranormal individuals who kill humans, or other paranormal creatures, and risk our exposure. Some start off human. Those pledge their soul in duty. But, many were created by the God, and were never anything but a reaper. And when I say punish, I mean eliminate in most cases. Though they do help settle disputes between paranormals. Those usually don't end in elimination. Reapers are overly righteous, but not always right, in my opinion."

"So, why aren't we calling them now?"

"Because I can't tell if there is a live victim in there. I have proof now, but I cannot call someone in good conscience and wait around doing nothing."

"You were able to smell the blood from a couple of blocks away, but you can't tell how many are inside?" Turney asked, sounding bewildered.

Octavius huffed. "There is too much blood. I suppose you could add that to my list of vampire weaknesses. My instincts hyper-focus on blood. Too much of it makes them all screwed up. Basically, my senses are about as useful as yours are at the moment. It's harder to hear, smell, or sense anything besides the blood."

"I see...so what's the plan for catching this guy?"

"I'm stronger, among other things. Wendigos are essentially human, besides their insatiable hunger for meat, and a few other traits. Long lives, etc." Octavius hummed before adding, "They are stronger than humans, though. You may want to watch out."

Turney's eyes narrowed. "So, there is no plan."

"I never said you had to come," Octavius snapped. Humans and their planning—so cautious.

"Let me be clear, I'm not standing out here alone waiting for you, or running away like a coward. I just want a clear answer. There is no plan, right?"

Octavius pouted. "Fine, there is no plan. Now, enough talk. We've wasted too much time already."

"Fine, lead the way." Turney waved him on irritably.

Tossing his head back on a hmph, Octavius marched forward to the front of the building. But, he thought better of his path and started off towards the right side of the paper mill, hoping to find a side door inside. The front door would be too dramatic. He wanted to be a little dramatic, not a lot. It was, in Octavius' opinion, essential to balance these types of things.

The chain-link fence was easy enough to get over. Octavius was rather impressed by how fast Turney made it over...as if he had done it many times before.

Over the fence, they walked around the right of the building and found the way blocked by a large white shipping container. It appeared oddly new. No wear or rust.

"Looks like this way is blocked," Turney muttered.

Octavius ignored him and examined the container. It was at least ten feet tall. There was no gap to the left of the container due to it being flush against the metal fence. And there was no way to hop the fence and go around because of how close the building next door was. He probably could have slipped through, if he changed into bat form or something smaller—but that would have meant leaving Turney behind.

There was a small gap on the side nearest the mill. Through that small gap, Octavius spotted a door.

He smiled at having found a way in, only to frown when he saw what hung between. Wires, giant conduits, and other cables sprouted out from holes in the container that had obviously been cut and sealed, and they ran directly through similar holes cut into the side of the building.

Interesting...very interesting. No matter, they had a way in.

"There's a door," Octavius announced happily.

"With no way to get to it," Turney rasped. "Why don't we just go in the front?"

GET IT TOGETHER

"No, no. Too dramatic. And we can get to it easily."

Without much thought, Octavius jumped up gently enough to catch the top edge of the container with both hands, and hoisted himself up.

"See, it's easy," Octavius said, smiling. Hands on his hips, he turned to stare down at Turney.

Why did Turney suddenly look so baffled? Or was he angry? His right eye appeared to be twitching. Octavius really was struggling with these human emotions. Maybe he should get a book or something?

Turney sighed, started to talk, then stopped, and sighed again. "Octavius, even if I was a good jumper, I wouldn't be able to make that."

Octavius' shoulders slumped—right.

Feeling put out, Octavius jumped down nimbly. Without asking, he grabbed Turney around the waist. Picking him up with one arm, Octavius repeated his jump. He hoisted himself up with one arm this time, while holding a panicking squirming human in the other.

Once on top, he stated, "See, no big deal."

"Some warning!" Turney whispered angrily.

"Sorry," Octavius demurred—he wasn't sorry.

Turney had quite a body hidden under those ill-fitting clothes. Arm still around the man, he smirked at the sound of Turney's speeding heartbeat. There was another reaction, but Octavius figured he'd best ignore the twitch against his hip, for the sake of their work relationship.

"Turney, your heart is beating rather fast."

"I thought you couldn't sense anything!?" the human snapped, cheeks heating up with all that delicious blood.

"You are pressed against me. How could I not feel it?" He smirked with a raised brow, choosing to be quite vague about what it was he was feeling—Turney was too fun to tease.

Turney spluttered, face flushing redder. The human's thumping heartbeat was speeding along even faster, and there was a much more noticeable twitch against his hip.

Chuckling, he ignored Turney's sputtering, and jumped down with him in his arm. Once on the other side, Octavius set the man down. Turney stumbled a few steps away, appearing to be trying to calm himself—cute.

Approaching the door, he put his ear against it and listened. Just like when they were standing in front, there was too much blood for his brain to move past it. He was basically stuck in human mode. Going inside would not be pleasant.

Oh, well. Octavius grabbed the handle and broke the door with a quick jerk of strength upon finding it locked.

The minute the door was open, the smell of blood and meat surged forward, attacking all of his senses to the point he felt dizzy and hesitant to enter. There was also an undeniable chill. Turney shuddered beside him, telling him the chill was more than just a quick breeze. Shaking his head, he pushed the dizzy feeling away.

Nose wrinkling in disgust, Octavius boldly walked inside, not bothering to hide. On the other hand, Turney was crouched and ferreting from one abandoned machine to another.

Octavius paused, baffled at the shifty human. "What are you doing?"

"Why are you talking so loud?" Turney whispered harshly. "And out in the open?"

"Wendigos have excellent hearing. He would have heard us as soon as we were at the container."

At his words, Turney's shoulders stiffened. "You can't be freaking serious," the human huffed harshly, before straightening from his hunch and stepping out from behind one of the machines.

This time Octavius could read the emotions Turney aimed his way. Definitely anger. The narrowed eyes and clenched jaw were good clues. He may have found the expression slightly funny.

Turney took a deep breath and let it out, the irritation seeming to float away. But it instantly returned when the man snapped, "These are the type of things you should tell me!"

Octavius suppressed the urge to say, *then maybe you should have asked.* He figured it wouldn't end well. Instead, he just shrugged and started walking again. It's not like Octavius kept it to himself on purpose. He just hadn't realized it was something Turney would want to know, or would need to know.

"It's like a fridge in here," Turney complained beside him, rubbing his arms as if to protect himself from the chill. "And it kind of smells like one," the human added.

He would have to take Turney's word for it on how cold it was. Because while he could feel the cool air, he was a lousy judge on it degree-wise.

"Wendigo, wendigo, come out and play!" Octavius yelled, as he stepped around a corner. The smell of blood now was all he could really pick up. It was so thick in the air, Octavius could barely tell that Turney was still next to him.

As his eyes took in the sight, the source of the smell, Octavius clicked his tongue. "What a mess."

"Oh my God." Turney swore heavily before asking, "Are

those—" Turney started gagging before he could finish his question.

"Bodies? Yes."

THE FACTORY HAD ESSENTIALLY BEEN TURNED into a giant refrigerator. While the previous parts had been left untouched, with machines left over from before the paper mill closed, this section had been long cleared out.

In its place was a gruesome display all around. Turney wanted to step back, his mind screaming to run, thinking this must be a nightmare. It was like stepping into a horror movie. As his gaze darted around the room, he found there was no safe place to look.

Even closing his eyes left no reprieve. The overwhelming copper and meat smell, and the constant dripping sounds, would not let him escape reality. Though calling what he saw meat was... Turney shuddered.

Table after long, cheap, plastic folding table—six in total—were dissecting the room. Turney thought they must have been white at one point, but they were stained in so much blood they were a speckled brown color. Each currently held a nude, lifeless body—or part of one. Some were missing limbs, but all of them were bloodless, with large, pale gashes over every major artery. A bloody electrical cart with saws sat nearby.

Octavius moved ahead of him towards it all. Turney's inner panic at what he saw had him taking shallow breaths through his mouth. Desperately trying to stop himself from freaking out.

Oh God, it wasn't working. Each breath in, the copper smell intensified. Hugging himself, he gripped his arms with trembling hands, trying to build up his courage to look at the rest of the horrors in the room. For the tables were not even the worst part. Stumbling forward, he peered upward at the source of the constant dripping.

The real horror hung from the rafters. Clothed bodies on hooks, people...what used to be people, hung upside down from their feet. The hook was through...flesh. Deep, bloody gouges that constantly dripped—fresh blood. There were seven of them. Turney began to flinch at each drip. Some made it into the buckets full of blood underneath, but much of it splattered on the ground.

As a blood drop splattered in front of him, Turney stepped back and almost stumbled over a plastic container. Right, the unknown element in this factory of horror—the randomly placed plastic containers filled with what looked like mounds of salt.

They were littered on the ground everywhere, but in a way that none of the dripping blood hit them. Glancing down at the unknown, Turney found himself almost robotically crouching in front of the one he almost tripped over.

Gulping, cold sweat dripping down his face, he hesitantly leaned closer to the white crystal pile. He let out a relieved breath when he discovered he'd been correct. It was salt. That relief drained away as his breath sent the top of the pile tumbling, revealing a bloodless face crusted with salt—the mouth gaping in a permanent silent scream, with the eyes missing.

"Fuck!" Turney stumbled backward, landing on his ass. He began to gag, bile rising up as his hands came in contact with the cold, sticky floor. The real meltdown hit when something warm and wet dropped onto his head. Turney released a startled cry, completely freaking out as the surprisingly warm blood dripped down his face.

Scrambling to his feet, Turney desperately swiped at the blood with his sleeves, and then wiped his hands on his pants. Dark red stains spread across his khakis and white dress shirt. Heart racing, he stared at his shaking hands that were still stained with blood.

Octavius eyed him with raised brows, but approached the container nearest and dug around it as if it was nothing. Turney grimaced when the male pulled out a leg. It was bloodless like the face, and just as crusted with salt. Seeing the whole thing, Turney noticed the cut marks were the same as those on the bodies on the tables that had missing limbs.

Fuck...were they trying to dry them out? For what purpose...? Turney did not want to know. Or rather, he didn't want to dwell on it, since it was clear it had to do with eating.

His gaze flicked back to the bodies on the tables. Eyeing one body to the next, Turney gasped when his eyes landed on the table dead center.

He had been wrong. Not all were lifeless. The woman on the table was tied up but still breathing. Her clothing, white in color, meant his eyes had skipped over her at first.

Turney went to tell Octavius about her, but the vampire spoke before he could.

"Come out, or I'll destroy your freezers, wendigo. Just think, all that meat would go to waste."

Meat—oh, that was worded so wrong. Wait...freezers? The whole building was a damn freezer. Yet...warm enough for blood to keep flowing.

Looking past all the gore, towards the direction Octavius was now facing, he finally noticed the large steel freezers lining the back wall. The urge to run returned.

How many bodies did they have stored?! Was this just the 'before' storage area? There were so many dead already.

Turney flinched at a deep growl, heart speeding up in anger and fear at the sight of Mr. Dietrich coming from behind one of the freezers. The male looked about the same. Besides the glowing yellow demon eyes—were those claws?

Turney let out a yelp of surprise when something small and hard poked him in the back. The yelp turned into a gargled choke, as an arm wrapped around his throat, cutting off part of his air supply and holding him in place. Then there was a clicking sound that he had only heard in movies, but instantly it told him about his current predicament.

"Don't do anything stupid, vampire, or I'll shoot your human friend. Unlike you, it's doubtful he'd survive being riddled with holes." The voice near his ear was gravely and deep. Based on the clawed hand on the arm holding him, he was going to guess it came from another nasty, human-eating wendigo.

Chapter Nine

To Dumb Decisions

"Here's the plan, vampire. You are going to do nothing as Leon ties you up. If you try anything, I'll kill him," the second wendigo stated succinctly.

Octavius' gaze narrowed at the other male, but remained unmoving. This other wendigo was much older—ancient for his kind. None of what he was wearing informed him of this, for the male's clothes were regular enough—jeans and a black t-shirt. Nor did his smell, or the general feel he had about him, for Octavius' senses were still fucked up from the blood. Really, it was just the look in the male's eyes. His eyes were ancient, as if he had seen more than others. It felt the same as when Octavius looked into his own eyes in the mirror.

The wendigo was, of course, not as old as Octavius. The maximum age for a wendigo was about nine hundred to a thousand years. This male looked to be in his early fifties, if using human age. Wrinkles were beginning to set in, and his hair was almost gray. If Octavius were to guess, the wendigo was probably close to seven-hundred-years-old. He would assume the male was nearing a growth cycle, where his body would age further—and make him look closer to sixty to anyone human.

Octavius stayed still as the younger wendigo tied him up with multiple, very thick chains. He could break them, but they meant escaping would take a few minutes longer.

To be honest, Octavius wasn't very surprised there was more than one wendigo. He already assumed there would be more, given how many humans had disappeared. Octavius did suspect that these two were not working alone. The body count in the building alone would suggest that.

"Sit!" Leon commanded.

Octavius glared at the little twirp before glancing down at the floor and back up again. "I'd rather stand, thank you."

"Sit, or I'll put a bullet in your human's skull," the older wendigo snapped.

He'd have to burn these pants, Octavius thought with irritation as he sat on the filth-covered floor.

Leon cackled. "Good boy! You'd make a nice pet."

"Boy...p-pet," Octavius choked on the words—this pissant little shit.

"It appears you've left him speechless. Good, for I need you to listen very carefully. Let me make this perfectly clear. The only way your human makes it out of here alive is if you listen to all we say," the older wendigo stated, as he finished tying up a dejected-looking Turney with rope.

The human was dragged over and sat down next to him. Eying him, Octavius began to think he was wrong. Maybe dejected wasn't the right word—more like shell shocked?

Perhaps Turney had been right. Maybe Octavius should

have come up with a plan. Like, what to do if they got caught.

At least then, Turney would have known they were in no danger. *Oh, he was so going to get scolded by the human later,* Octavius thought with a pout.

"Why should the human go free?" Leon asked, sounding irritated at the idea. The younger wendigo crouched down in front of Turney, his face transformed entirely as he leaned in and took a breath. Yellow eyes sinking into his skull, the wendigo's skin paled. The bones of his face jutted out, his chin now coming to a harsh point while his mouth widened. His teeth lengthened to dangerous points.

Turney blanched, lips twisting in disgust, as he tried to lean his face away.

"Leave it alone, Leon," the elder growled.

"Aw, but, Master, he smells especially sweet. Besides, don't we deserve him for all the losses we are about to suffer?"

"Fuck you," Turney growled.

Leon's face twisted to become even uglier, but a smirk soon appeared. Not that it made the creature any more appealing. Leon's yellow gaze swept down Turney in a way that made Octavius very nervous.

"How about I fuck you instead?" The male's long black tongue slipped out and swiped across Turney's blood-stained cheek. "One last bit of pleasure before I drain you dry and consume you."

"Get away from him!" Octavius hissed at the wendigo. How dare he touch what didn't belong to him?!

Glancing at Turney in worry, Octavius' eyes widened in surprise when he found instead of horror or panic, Turney's eyes were hard with raw fury. The human's jaw clamped so tightly, you could see a muscle twitching.

A wealth of pride warmed Octavius' heart at how strong his precious human was being.

Leon must have seen the defiance as well, for the male growled. But, whatever he'd intended to do never came to fruition, for the older wendigo grabbed his arm and hauled him upwards.

In Octavius's opinion, it was the smartest move the older male had made today. Of course, the best move would have been to abandon Leon and flee while he still could. But, it was way too late for that now. Octavius would never let either of them get away after this—especially not Leon.

"Child, let me make this very clear. You take what's mine, and I will make every last second of your short life painful beyond imagination," Octavius threatened with a sweet smile.

While he may have just met Turney, the human was now his employee, and he had already determined that they would become close friends. That made him Octavius' human. It made him someone he had to protect. Octavius was not willing to give that future friendship up. Also, where on earth would he find a better driver?

"You—" Leon started, taking a step towards him in obvious rage.

"Enough, Leon! He is older and stronger than he looks. The only reason he hasn't attacked us is because of the human. So, it will stay living, and you will not touch it. Now, start bringing in the things from the truck. We must quickly salvage what we can, while we can."

"But, Jory—"

"Go!" the wendigo he now knew was named Jory, snarled.

Not that his name mattered much to Octavius. He, along with his pupil, would be dead soon enough.

Leon disappeared around the corner, and Jory faced him.

"Sorry about that. The youth remain as ambitious and rowdy as always. Now, I know you haven't called any reapers yet." Jory smirked and paused.

The male probably thought Octavius was regretting his own actions—he wasn't. So, Octavius stared blankly as if he didn't have a care in the world.

When his expression didn't change, to Jory's evident disappointment, the male continued. "I actually arrived a bit after you and heard some of your conversation. So, yes, I know you didn't call anyone, and that no one is on their way to save you. Don't even try to lie about it. Now, you will sit there while we collect what is ours, and allow us to safely leave with it all."

Octavius decided to play along, as if he intended to let either leave. "I want the other living human as well. The young girl."

Jory rolled his eyes. "It is yours. Too much of a hassle to bring with us right now anyway."

The wendigo picked up a large black bag off the floor and started to go around plucking limbs out of the plastic containers. The male made quick work of it, and once full, Jory zipped the bag and set it down carefully.

Picking up a second large, empty black bag, the male walked over to the first freezer. The latch made a noise as it was flicked open, and Octavius couldn't help but grimace as he got a look inside the first freezer. They had wrapped individual parts, like a butcher would, some were even vacuum-sealed. Stack after stack. Torsos, heads, legs, and arms, all in various sizes—so many dead...

"Hah..." Turney chuckled softly. "I'm going to die for twenty dollars and some photocards."

Octavius rolled his eyes—his dramatic human had returned. Had Turney not just heard what the wendigo said about not killing him? Also, the man seemed really resentful towards Octavius' photocards. Well, too bad, as he was not sharing—hmph.

Shifting a bit on the hard floor, Octavius grimaced at the feeling of his pants sticking. Okay, time to speed things up. He wanted off this disgusting floor, as much, if not more so than Turney.

"Hey, wendigo. How old do you think I am?"

Octavius saw Turney eye him out of the corner of his eye, giving him a 'what are you doing?' kind of look.

Jory hesitated for a moment at his question, but didn't look back. He just grabbed a pre-packaged limb and shoved it into his bag, stating harshly, "I don't have time for your games, vampire."

"Aw, it will be quick, I promise," Octavius whined. In that instant, he slipped back into 'super vamp' mode and repeated his question. "Now, how old do you think I am?"

The mode made the blood smell unbearable, instantly giving him a massive headache, but he'd live.

Clearly irritated, the male spun around and froze on the spot upon seeing him. "Shit!" Jory took off.

Or at least, he tried to. Octavius slipped into the male's mind, forcing him to stop running and to calmly walk back.

"Oh, fuck..." Turney gasped.

While his puppet master power did not work on most

paranormals, wendigos were similar enough to humans that they were not included in the majority.

He commanded Jory to crouch down right in front of him. Glancing into the other's eyes, he could see the panic, the fear, and then the hatred. That was the one thing about puppet mode, Octavius could control what they did, what they said, and their facial expression, but not the look in their eyes. What was the quote about eyes...that they were the window to the soul? Perhaps it was true. Either way, their thoughts were their own. Octavius did feel what they were feeling, but had no knowledge of specifics.

"My dear, Jory. You made a huge mistake, didn't you?" Octavius tsked. "You underestimated my age. You should have run when you saw me. Or, at the very least, assess what I could do first. It is actually funny that you arrived early enough to eavesdrop on our conversation about reapers." Octavius giggled. "But not soon enough to see the red in my eyes when we first arrived. Fate was not on your side."

"Y-you..." Turney stuttered.

Octavius met Turney's probing gaze. "I'll explain later, promise. Just know everything is going to be okay. However, right now, I need you to put on your best acting skills when Leon gets back. Pretend to still be scared, like you are going to die. I need him close enough to grab him, but first I need him to do something for me."

Turney's brows drew together. A variety of emotions filtered across his expression, too fast for Octavius to identify. Eventually, the man nodded in agreement. He didn't say anything, but it was good enough.

Octavius sent Jory back to doing what he had been doing and stayed sitting on the icky, icky ground, waiting for the little bastard who had called him a boy to return. It was an annoyingly long wait. It took Leon at least twenty minutes to come back carrying a large red freezer chest and what appeared to be far too many empty body bags.

On his return, Octavius closed his eyes to hide the red. At the same time, he had Jory stop what he was doing to face Leon and give him an order. "Call the others, have them meet at your house in an hour. Tell them we may be late."

"Are you sure..." He could tell the younger wendigo was frowning, based on his tone. "Shouldn't we—"

"Do it!" Octavius had Jory yell.

"Fine!"

Octavius wondered if Leon saw the anger in Jory's eyes. Had he mistaken it for anger at him, instead of anger at being controlled?

Leon did what he was told, and quickly at that. The male called three others, telling them to meet up. Minutes after the last phone call ended, Octavius stood up, unwilling to stay seated on the floor any longer.

"Sit down or—"

"Or what, junior? You will shoot my human? I think not," Octavius mocked. He met the other's gaze. Leon's eyes widened, but returned to normal as Octavius took over his body.

He marched both wendigos over to stand in front of him. Octavius smiled brightly at the two. "Leon, why don't you untie my dear Turney. Jory, you unchain me." He put power into his voice to make them follow his orders.

Turney was freed much sooner than he was. The single rope they had tied the human up with took much less effort to remove than the multiple chains that were around Octavius. His human stretched and sighed at being freed—very at peace. Happy was the word that had entered

Octavius' thoughts, until Turney took a swing at Leon, punching him right on the mouth.

Leon went down, unable to do anything to protect himself or cushion his fall, due to being under Octavius' control. Octavius' eyes widened at the sudden act of violence.

"Fuck you!" Turney growled. "Thinking you are owed people's lives, their bodies!? They had as much right as you did to live. You are owed nothing, and I hope your last moments are as painful as I think they will be." Turney spun, turning to look at Jory. "And YOU! It? I'm an *it* now? Says the monsters chopping up people and munching on them!"

The last of the chains on Octavius dropped and Turney stepped forward menacingly, looking as if he was about to punch Jory as well.

"Wait!" Octavius yelled, as Turney's arm swung back. He grabbed Turney's wrist and easily brought his fist forward, even though he resisted. "Calm down. There is no need to make your fist bleed even more for such trash. No point risking infection. They both will suffer before they die, that I can promise you."

TURNEY GLANCED down at his fist, shocked to find that his knuckles were indeed bleeding. "I…" He trailed off, feeling the urge to fight leave him.

Octavius gave him a gentle smile and patted his hand, as

if to assure him things were going to be okay, before releasing Turney's wrist.

"While I chain them up, why don't you check on the young woman tied up on the table? Make sure she isn't hurt. Don't try to wake her up, though...this would be a bit frightening to see, I'd imagine."

A bit frightening, he says!? Hah! Turney was sure to have nightmares. So, yeah, her not waking up until she was out of here would probably be for the best.

Turney weaved through the buckets, and containers of horror, heading towards the table dead center in the room. His shoes stuck a bit to the ground as he walked, the blood thicker the further he went.

Looking down at the girl, she appeared young, as in teenager young, which was horrifying to him—God, they even went after children. The thing was, she didn't seem to be the type of person Veronica had stated were the victims.

This girl was fully dressed—thank fuck for that—but her clothes were brand name, and while her long brown hair was not dyed, it had definitely been styled recently. Glancing her over, Turney tried to see if she was hurt without actually touching her. Luckily, it seemed that besides the ropes and the stained white table holding her up, she was just sleeping. No wounds in sight—breathing nice and even.

Turney sighed in relief before he turned around and called back softly, "She's unharmed, just sleeping."

"I'm guessing they gave her something to keep her out for a while," Octavius mused, as he finished chaining both Leon and Jory together.

The two shuffled and sat down, right where Turney and Octavius had been sitting. Relief that this was essentially over hit him hard, and his knees almost gave way. Catching himself on the edge of the girl's table, Turney took a calming breath before slowly making his way back over to Octavius.

This had to be the longest, most insane, mind-blowing day he had ever had. Turney felt both emotionally and physically drained.

Vampires, zombies, Gods, wendigos, and reapers. Turney checked his watch—4:26—six hours ago he hadn't even known any of them actually existed. Now, here he was, helping a vampire—who had a zombie for a secretary—capture human-eating wendigos, so they could be given to some random God-created reapers for punishment. Which God, Turney didn't know, as apparently there was more than one. All this while covered in blood stains, surrounded by dead bodies and people parts that the said wendigos planned to munch on.

Turney honestly needed a long, hot shower, and to take a nap...and possibly something to wipe his brain clean.

Holy fuck—the vampire he was helping could also control minds. Something he hadn't been told earlier. Octavius hadn't used it on him, had he?

No...no...of course not. Octavius didn't seem like the type of person to want to control anyone. Besides, there hadn't been a moment where Turney hadn't been in control of his body. He'd been in emotional distress, caused by Octavius, but he hadn't been controlled into that distress. Octavius couldn't have. He was sure he'd remember if the vampire's eyes went red, followed by him losing all control of his bodily functions.

Shaking his head at the thought, Turney sighed and asked, "What now?"

Octavius, who had taken out his phone and had been fiddling with it for the last few minutes, looked up. "Now?

Now I send this text to the reapers, and we wait for instructions." The male made a show of tapping his screen to send said text.

"Text? Wouldn't calling be faster?" Turney asked, almost choking on his words with how truly exasperated he felt.

Octavius bottom lip popped out. "But I don't want to talk to them. And I already typed it all up and hit send." The vampire held up his phone, the screen showing a long text that had been successfully sent, as if it made what he was saying any less crazy.

Turney could feel a headache build. "If there is no reply in the next ten minutes, please call them."

"Fine! I will...in ten minutes!" Octavius snapped, looking like a child being told to do something he didn't want to do.

Turney closed his eyes and went to rub them, then he remembered the blood. Sighing again, he let his hands drop to his sides. The headache seemed to have slid solidly forward at Octavius' whining.

Turney blinked his eyes open at the sound of a phone camera. That first fake shutter sound was followed by many, many, more.

Scanning the room, he found Octavius no longer standing there, but running around like a mad man, snapping pictures.

"What are you doing?!" Turney spluttered.

Octavius took another picture before looking over at him, seeming as confused as Turney currently felt. "I'm getting proof?"

"Proof for what?!"

"Our case, of course! How are we supposed to be paid if I don't have proof?"

"The little girl does not need to see all of this!" Turney gasped in horror, and waved his hands in panic, at the thought of Octavius showing Veronica pictures of mutilated bodies. "Just take pictures of Leon chained up or something! Besides, him not returning should be proof enough."

Octavius shook his head and huffed, "Fine," as if Turney was the one being unreasonable, before stomping over and taking pictures of the two wendigos.

Chapter Ten

A Lack Of Communication

About thirty minutes later, Octavius announced they could leave. Turney had many questions, but decided to wait until they got back to the car. He was too tired to think beyond the clean clothes he knew were stashed in his trunk. Thank fuck he kept a bag full of gym clothes in his trunk. It made going to the gym at the last moment possible. Or, like in this case, it meant he could get out of his blood-covered clothing.

The walk back to the car added to his exhaustion, and he couldn't help but feel relief at the sight of his baby—it luckily had not been towed or broken into.

Upon reaching it, Turney revealed, "I have some extra clothes in the trunk... They should fit you, but definitely won't be your style. There are wet wipes as well."

While Octavius wasn't as filthy as Turney was, the vampire had still sat on the sticky, blood-coated floor the same as he had. No way in hell did he want any of that shit on his seats.

"I just need pants. I'm afraid anything with blood on it

will have to be burned. It's evidence, you see. Nothing can be left behind."

"Won't be a problem. I don't want to wear any of it again anyway."

Popping the trunk, the first thing he grabbed was the large package of wet wipes. Flipping the lid, he plunked a few out and used them to scrub the blood from his hands. It stung over his cut knuckles, but he'd survive. He tossed the used ones into a random plastic shopping bag he found in his trunk. Hands as clean as they could be at the moment, he dragged his black duffle bag closer, unzipped it, and pulled out a set of clothes for himself, and bottoms for Octavius.

The lack of a place to change meant both would have to undress in the open. Turney prayed no one would come by because ending the day on public indecency charges would have sucked. At least the small lot was blocked in by empty buildings on all sides, with only a small opening onto a street. They'd been lucky no one had spotted them on the way back to the car. The bloodstains would have been hard to explain.

Back to Octavius, Turney kicked off his shoes and stripped down—tossing all of his clothes to the ground. In only his boxer briefs and socks, Turney quickly pulled on a tightly fitted red t-shirt and gray joggers. He was about to slip his dress shoes back on when he remembered the sticky floors. Sighing, Turney dug back into the duffle bag and pulled out a pair of black tennis shoes.

"Our shoes are contaminated as well," Turney pointed out as he slipped the sneakers on and turned around.

Octavius had already changed into the loose-fitting joggers, which looked out of sorts with his jacket, vest, and tie.

Turney blinked in confusion on noticing the vampire's

appreciative gaze. Narrowing his eyes, he huffed, "You looked, didn't you?"

"Was...I supposed to turn away?" Octavius asked with a brow raised.

"It would have been the polite thing to do!" Turney snapped, feeling heat rise on his neck.

"Sorry."

Turney snorted. "Your shoes."

"I'll just use the wipes."

"Are you sure?"

"I doubt you have an extra pair of shoes in there that would fit me."

He stared at the man's feet. Octavius' feet were definitely bigger. A wandering thought floated through: *Where else could the vampire be bigger?* But, Turney shoved it aside.

He spent the next ten minutes helping Octavius clean the bottoms of his shoes. Turney then had to stand there silently, trying not to blush, as Octavius cleaned the blood off his face and out of his hair.

All clean, and now less likely to get arrested if pulled over, they shoved all the soiled clothes and wipes into the shopping bag and left it in the trunk.

Turney slipped into the driver's seat with a groan, feeling the weight of everything slamming down on him in the form of even more exhaustion.

"Are you sure it's okay to just leave them there? Not to mention the young girl on the table? What if she wakes up before the reaper or reapers get here?" he asked, as Octavius slid into the passenger seat and put on his seatbelt.

"It's fine," the vampire assured him. "The reapers texted me they had arrived at both locations and would take care of the wendigos and the young girl. They will make sure she returns home safely."

After the day he had, it took a moment for Turney's mind to process what Octavius had said. It all amounted to a lot of what the fucks. Irritated as all hell, Turney faced forward to stop himself from giving in to the urge to scream. Angrily he shoved his seatbelt on and started the car.

Facing forward still, he fell into a rant. "Again, this is the type of information you are supposed to tell the people you are working with. There was a major issue with communication in this case. For instance, the mind control thing. Would have been nice to know. Not to mention that wendigos had far-reaching hearing."

When his words were met with silence, he glanced over at Octavius, only to find him looking down, typing rapidly on his phone.

"Are you even listening to me?" Turney fumed, voice raising in volume.

Octavius' fingers stilled on the phone, and the vampire looked over at him wide-eyed. "Were you speaking?"

"YES!" Turney bellowed. "You know, for having such good hearing, you sure as hell seem to miss a lot."

The vampire's hands dropped into his lap, and his eyes widened further, his bottom lip popping out. "It's not on purpose," Octavius whined.

GET IT TOGETHER

IT REALLY WASN'T on purpose...well, not all the time. There were moments, Octavius supposed, that he chose not to listen. But really, a lot of it was just his inability to focus on doing multiple things at once. For instance, reading and holding a conversation at the same time—not possible. Or, in this case, texting and hearing someone else physically talking to him. Octavius would admit his attention span was tenuous at best.

Seeing Turney's expression, he deepened his pout—oh, no, his human was mad at him. How did he fix it?

Turney's eyes narrowed, but the man took a deep breath, and all the anger seemed to seep from him. His expression was now more exasperated than angry.

Octavius gave him a smile, trying to look small and innocent.

"Fine, I get it. You can't help it." Turney sighed, before muttering under his breath softly, "I'll just get used to repeating myself, no big deal."

Octavius was going to assume, admitting he heard that loud and clear would backfire on him, so he pretended he heard nothing.

"So, my dear Turney, best driver in the world...tell me, what is wrong?" Octavius asked, laying on the sweetness and charm.

Turney snorted. "Well, the main issue is the lack of communication. And me not being told information I should know. Like the fact that wendigos have good hearing."

"I mean, it is why I needed you to draw Leon away from the house."

"It was a miracle I even managed to get him out of the—" Turney's eyes narrowed again, making Octavius rather nervous. "You knew Mr. Dietrich would know how to fix a car, didn't you?"

Octavius scrunched down in his seat under the accusing look. "Well, you see. It was in the background information my contact emailed to me."

"And you didn't share this with me because...?"

"I didn't think about it?" Octavius would concede he probably should have at least shared that information with Turney, considering he'd been helping him with the ruse.

"What about the mind control thing?" Turney huffed.

"Well, you didn't ask," Octavius cried. "How was I supposed to know you'd want to know? It's not like I can read minds—" Octavius let out a surprised "oh" on remembering that he actually could read minds.

"You can read minds too?!" Turney gasped accusingly.

"I mean, I can only read human minds, and only when I'm in 'super vamp' mode."

"'Super vamp' mode..."

"You know when I have the red eyes? It's officially called phasing, but that was such a boring name that I renamed it. Anyway, it takes a lot of concentration, and I have to touch the individual." Octavius paused and tapped his lips at the thought of doing it. "Honestly, it's a bigger pain than it's worth. I don't really do it much."

He avoided phasing unless he had to. Octavius' disinterest in using most 'super vamp' mode abilities was probably the reason he had a headache every time he did use them. Disuse and all that.

Turney sighed heavily, sounding eerily like Scarlett—not in tone, but how deep it seemed to go—and banged his head lightly on the steering wheel. Turney then curiously remained slumped there.

GET IT TOGETHER

Hmm—that can't be too comfortable, could it? Octavius' head cocked—why would one lay in such a place?

Turney suddenly jerked back up to look at him. Octavius flinched in shock, accidentally flinging his phone onto the dashboard.

Wide-eyed, Octavius smiled at him weakly, blindly reaching for his phone on the dash, not daring to turn away.

"Can you please just promise me this one thing?" Turney begged.

Octavius nodded enthusiastically, phone back in hand. "Yes. Of course. What is it?"

"If there is any, and I mean any, information that could potentially save, harm, or influence my actions, can you please tell me?"

That seemed reasonable enough—for anyone except him, as he tended to not always understand what would be considered important for others...but he could try, right? "I'll try my best," Octavius said with fake confidence.

"Thank you," Turney said before rubbing his head, as if he was in pain. "Where to now?"

"Back to Franklin Fairwood Park," Octavius announced, happy that Turney's scolding had ended.

TURNEY PARKED in the exact same spot he had pulled into earlier that day and watched again as Octavius jumped out of the car, softly screaming in excitement, "My babies."

Now, while he would admit—to himself—it was sort of

cute, Turney was so drained that the fact Octavius was being cute couldn't soften his irritation at being awake at the moment.

The vampire practically ran across the pebbled ground, to reach the far bench where the little girl, Veronica, was sitting.

Now nearing 6pm, Turney was again struck by how quiet and empty the park was. It was summer, where the hell were all the kids?

His eyes widened when Octavius pulled out what he thought may be his phone—hard to tell from this distance.

Octavius...wouldn't actually... Nope, the vampire was definitely showing the little girl something on his phone. Surely it was just the photos of Leon, right? No way would the vampire expose a twelve-year-old to dismembered bodies. Haha—sure, Octavius had a few screws loose, but surely he wouldn't go that far.

The thought did occur to him that Octavius had taken the photos in the first place to show her. So, Turney probably should not have felt the least bit confident that he wouldn't show her the ones he managed to take before being stopped.

He stared at them narrowly—she didn't appear to be freaking out. That had to be a good sign, right?

The two separated, no longer staring at Octavius' phone. Veronica pulled something out of her pink backpack and handed it over to Octavius. Judging by the ear-piercing squeal of happiness that he heard next, Turney assumed it was the remaining BTS photocards.

The two shook hands, and Octavius made his way back to the car with a skip in his step. The vampire got in, quickly shut the door, and buckled up. He then just sat there staring at the cards in his hands, as if in a trance.

Judging this to be a moment where if Turney spoke, he would not be heard, he tapped Octavius on the shoulder.

At the tap, the vampire's head slowly turned to face him. "Yes?"

Octavius' eyes were literally glowing, and Turney would have sworn they sparkled. It was a bit shocking how happy the cards made him. Then again, Turney supposed he was much the same when around cars.

"You didn't show her those bloody, gory images, did you?" he asked, almost jokingly.

Octavius gave him a wide-eyed blink, his head cocking in a way that made his stomach drop. "I did. Why do you ask?"

"She's a little girl," Turney yelled shrilly. He covered his face with his hands, groaning. "You've probably scarred her for life. I know I'll be having a nightmare or two."

"Turney, how old do you think Veronica is?" Octavius hummed.

Turney's hands dropped from his face to the wheel at the question, and he met Octavius' obviously amused gaze. Why did such a simple question sound like a trap?

"Maybe twelve at most, or around there?"

Octavius burst into a fit of giggles. "No wonder you were questioning so much. Answer this, why did Leon cover up his scent?"

"Because there were other paranormals around him?"

Turney frowned and then suddenly remembered the way she said the words 'he is not human' when speaking about Leon. They'd been so sure…and the only way they could be that sure is… "She's not human!?"

Octavius smiled at him as if he did something cute. "No, she is not. I mean, think about it, Turney. Who better to know when one had gone rogue than one's own kind. In her parents' case, sometimes being busy and arrogant can make you ignore obvious signs."

"She's a wendigo too!?" Turney croaked, choking on air.

"A very young wendigo, but a wendigo nonetheless," the vampire mused. "But wendigos, as much as they are like humans, do not age like humans. While she may look like a twelve-year-old, she is already older than you. I'd say by at least twenty-five to thirty years."

"FIFTY! SHE'S OVER FIFTY?! Why the hell were we paid in photocards then!?" Turney raged, before simmering down to just a snap. "Wait, that's not even important. Why the hell didn't you tell me?"

Octavius looked at him like a deer in headlights at first, before a little head shake had his expression changing to defiance. "You seem very hung up on my photocards." The vampire held the new cards closer, as if fearing Turney would try to do something to them. "Either way, I imagine it would be hard to earn money while looking so young. Besides, she may be fifty, and probably more mentally mature than a human child, but her overall mindset would not quite have reached full maturity. Think of it this way; she is older, but everyone around her still treats her like any human would treat someone who looks twelve. She is still considered underaged to other wendigos, and they treat her as such. Therefore, her mindset is still that of a child's. A mature child with few childlike interests, yes, but still a child."

"Wait...how many wendigos are in this area?"

"I believe there's quite a large pod of them here. Why?"

No wonder the park was so abandoned during the middle of the fucking summer. Wait a minute...

"I noticed you conveniently skipped over how you did

not tell me that she was a wendigo," Turney drawled with a fake ass smile.

Octavius quickly glanced away to stare out the window and muttered, "I don't know what you mean."

Turney scoffed loudly. "Oh, you don't, do you? Didn't at all consider I may have trusted the information more if I had known it was from a fifty-year-old? Hell, knowing she was also a wendigo probably would have made me not even care about her age!"

Octavius slumped back in his seat, facing forward. His signature pout was out in full force. "I just didn't think about it, okay? It wasn't on purpose!"

The male was...infuriating. "Oh, my..." Turney groaned. "Oh, my head."

Chapter Eleven

Understanding Octavius

"Put it down!" Turney huffed in exasperation as he chased Octavius around the male's desk. Turney jumped forward, attempting to grab hold of the vampire, but Octavius easily evaded him.

"Never!" the vampire screamed, as he scurried away from him.

"Dammit, Octavius!" Turney slammed his hands on the desk, glaring at Octavius who was standing on the other side. "You know you can't eat it. Just put the sucker down," he warned, pointing at him.

"You don't know that!" the vampire cried defiantly, before sprinting towards Scarlett's desk.

Turney watched, baffled as the male's form shrunk down into a tiny bat. He burst out laughing at the ridiculousness of watching the tiny thing waddle, with a sucker clamped in its right claw, underneath the desk. Ridiculous, but still adorable.

Shaking his head, Turney walked over to the desk with a chuckle. He kneeled down and peered underneath. Octavius was hiding in the left corner, his giant black eyes glowing in the shadows. While there wasn't much light, he could still see that the bat was pouting.

"Octavius," he said gently, trying to coax the vampire out.

"No, it's mine!" Octavius squeaked.

The bat's eyes narrowed, and he could see the moment Octavius made a decision.

"Don't!"

Turney sighed as the vampire shoved the watermelon sucker into his tiny bat mouth.

"Mmm," the bat moaned in happiness.

And things were fine and dandy, right until the moment Octavius bit down. The crunch was followed by crying.

Teary-eyed, the bat opened his mouth. The now partly ash sucker fell out onto the carpeted floor.

"Bleh..." Octavius sobbed, as he tried to spit out the ash.

Sighing again, Turney scrunched down further and reached out, picking Octavius up. The vampire didn't fight or try to flee.

"This is why I told you not to."

Octavius sniffled and let out squeaking coughs. "B-but I thought it would work."

Turney carried the bat over to his desk and sat down, pulling the box of tissues closer to him. Setting Octavius down on his desk, Turney yanked out a few tissues and used them to wipe at the vampire's mouth. The bat spat and sputtered for the next few moments as he tried to rid his mouth and tongue of the ash.

"Well, it definitely won't work if you bite down, Octavius. And since you have bit down each and every time, I'm not sure why you keep trying."

It had been a week and a half since Turney had started

working there, and this was the third time the vampire had done this. Turney supposed it was partly his fault for having them on his desk. But, also not, as he had hidden them after the first incident, so it was on Octavius for being a snooping candy thief.

After wiping the bat's mouth with a clean tissue one last time, he tossed the used ones in the trash, grabbed his water bottle, and shoved it towards Octavius.

"Drink," Turney commanded.

Octavius climbed the bottle, wrapping his wings and claws around it as he started to drink.

There was no denying that it was adorable to watch. Turney just barely held back his 'aww' when Octavius released the bottle and let himself plop down onto the desk. The bat stared up at him, tears flowing now, and trembling in his upset.

"There, there," Turney said, picking Octavius up again with his right hand and gently rubbing the top of his fuzzy head with his left thumb.

Octavius, voice as high pitched as ever, whaled. "I did try to resist! But how can one not bite a lollipop?" The vampire then started to cling to Turney's right hand.

"I do understand. It would be tough for me to not bite as well." A thought occurred to him. "How about this...I'll try to find something that tastes like watermelon suckers, but in liquid form? And if I can't find something, I'll try to make something."

"Reeaally?" Octavius asked, the word drawn out. He sniffled, staring up at him with hope.

Turney chuckled. "Yes, really."

Octavius let out a contented, happy little sigh, relaxing in his hand as Turney continued to rub his head.

Turney was fully aware of how odd this was. Petting your boss was generally frowned upon—he would assume. But, Turney found it was an easy way to calm Octavius down. And the vampire changed into bat form a lot. All of it sounded like the perfect excuse for Turney to cave, giving in to his urges to cuddle and pet cute animals.

Octavius was just too cute for Turney to resist, and the whole reason his recent search history was full of bats and bat plushies. While he had deduced that the species of bat the vampire liked to turn into was the peter's dwarf epauletted fruit bat, he had yet to find a plush as cute as Octavius.

Turney's love of cute things may have become obsessive at this point in his life. At least, that is what many of his exes had claimed. Of course, most of them had judged him for his extensive plushie collection. How his interests didn't fit how he looked.

They saw his six-foot-tall and muscular frame, and assumed shit. Like, that Turney was a macho top, or that he would never bottom. Or that he liked sports and shit. Well, Turney wasn't a macho top, and he loved to bottom more than he wanted to top, and he hated all sports, besides racing. Turney was a six-foot-tall, muscly switch who loved to bottom, was in love with fast cars, plushies, cute animals, and his favorite color was pink.

He supposed it was his own fault. His love for cute meant he tended to gravitate towards very cute men. While he knew that just because they were small and cute, it didn't mean they were bottoms. Turney seemed to have the worst luck. Even when he stressed he was more of a bottom, somehow, they hadn't believed him.

It was a bit concerning, but Octavius was pushing a lot of

his buttons. The vampire was adorable, yet very fucking hot, and he could turn into cute animals.

His thumb froze when the door to the office opened. Spotting Scarlett, his back stiffened under her stare.

She shook her head as she eyed Turney. "Babying him again, I see."

Turney cleared his throat. "There was another sucker incident."

The redhead snorted. "You being so nice will just make him do it again."

Octavius jumped from his hands onto Turney's desk and made a hissing noise before sticking his tongue out at her.

Her eyes narrowed on him, but she didn't respond to the childishness. "Lilah's here with material samples."

Lilah being the woman Turney had been told was in charge of the renovations to the office. He'd seen the woman in passing, always seeming to leave as he arrived, but wasn't sure what she was. Turney could now confirm she was not human, as she didn't seem shocked at the sight of a small bat.

Octavius changed back. Slipping off Turney's desk, the vampire went to greet the other woman who'd appeared in the doorway after being announced.

Turney stared blankly out into the office. Laminate floors, white walls, and besides his added flimsy desk against the wall with a surprisingly decent desk chair, everything remained the same.

It had been over a week since Turney had discovered paranormal creatures existed. And he thought he was doing pretty okay, under the circumstances. Only one nightmare so far about wendigos and body parts, so there was that. Considering how chaotic and terrifying the first day had been, he really wanted to applaud his own ability to cope.

Though, coping had been much easier with the check he'd received the day after that first day. Over seven-hundred dollars, almost four-hundred of it had been a 'sorry you were almost eaten' bonus—Octavius' own words. No taxes had been taken out, so that was a bit of a pain. As was explaining that a paycheck directly deposited at the end of the week worked better than a handwritten check every day. Turney did have to say Octavius had lovely handwriting.

He was going to assume Scarlett had handled it, for he had received an accumulative direct deposit at the end of last week, with the taxes taken out—thank fuck.

What exactly he was currently being paid for he didn't know, as they hadn't worked a case since the first one. The hours were random. Sometimes nine to five, whereas other times he was here from 5pm to 1am. It really all depended on what time Octavius wanted him to come in, but he was usually there for at least eight hours each day.

It was currently 6pm, and the sun had set about an hour ago. He had been here since 1pm. All in all, Turney couldn't find it in himself to complain. He was essentially getting paid to sit around and play on his phone...and have the most bizarre conversations of his life with Octavius. Possibly, also attempting to stop the vampire from eating things he wasn't supposed to.

Turney had discovered that BTS' discography was actually meaningful and covered all genres. Of course, this was only after Octavius had forced him to watch hours of videos on *YouTube*—Turney rolled his eyes. The vampire was damn persistent.

Shaking the thought away, Turney picked up the newspaper he'd abandoned after noticing Octavius had stolen a sucker—again. He wasn't one to read the paper much, primarily due to not wanting to see all the horrible shit humanity was up to, but he was bored.

Scanning through the first article, which was about a community art project, he glanced down to the second headline and found his eyes widening. "Old Mill fire ruled accidental," he murmured aloud.

Holy shit—the article stated the Old Mill had burned entirely to the ground. Nothing but ashes were left. Staring at the picture below the headline, he had to say the description was apt. There was nothing left, just a pile of ash where the multi-story mill had once been—only the chain link fence remained intact. Which wouldn't make sense, as the shipping container was nowhere in sight, and if it had caught fire...well, it had been up close to the next building.

Reading further, he found that the fire inspector had ruled it an accident due to faulty wiring. No foul play was involved, despite how destructive the fire had been and how fast it spread. The fire spread due to the flammable materials left behind from when the mill had been abandoned. No other buildings in the area were affected.

How the hell does a building burn to complete ashes without an actual accelerant? Setting the paper down, he dug out his phone and quickly searched the news for any other fires in the last week. He chuckled at reading about a second fire on the same day, that also resulted in the complete destruction of a building. A house in Franklin. He paled, reading it had resulted in the death of the house owner, Leon Dietrich, and four other individuals. One with the first name, Jory. Unlike the mill, it had been ruled that Leon Dietrich had murdered the other four, before committing suicide and burning the house to the ground.

Well, damn, the reapers sure had taken care of business.

Turney took a deep breath and tried to see how he felt knowing he played a part in their deaths—even if he had not done it himself.

There was a feeling of unease there, a twisting in his stomach. But, when Turney examined the cause, he found it was not due to the deaths of the wendigos. What made his stomach twist was the idea of all those who had died at their hands—their families and friends never knowing what really happened. He understood the reason why they couldn't know. Though, had he been one of their victims...no one would be mourning or looking for him.

Did Octavius know about the fires? He glanced over at the vampire in question. Turney almost laughed when Octavius caught him staring and winked at him, before his attention went back to the designer.

Maybe at least one person would look for him if he disappeared.

Turney couldn't help but grin while he watched Octavius gesture wildly to the interior designer. Designer? Or was she an interior architect? The woman was of average height, had long black hair, sharp features, a clean, make-up-free appearance, and wore a dress suit.

This was not their first meeting, or even second. Some choices had been made and were being made—samples of various materials were spread out across Octavius' desk.

From previous conversations, Turney gathered that the original theme Octavius had intended on was spooky, to go along with the agency's name. Which explained the flyers, and possibly the boxes of black printer paper.

That idea had long since sailed off into the distance, and had been replaced, no doubt due to the designer's suggestions or perhaps enthusiastic willfulness to blurt out ideas. The woman was matching Octavius in hyperactivity and excited hand gestures.

So, now spooky was out, and a 1920s detective theme office was in. It still fit—kind of. It sounded like any who walked into the office in the future would feel like they had stepped into the past. Or were maybe surrounded by the undead?

Turney had no intention of trying to rationalize or question the change. The changes would definitely match how Octavius dressed—not so much anyone else. Scarlett, he supposed, wouldn't look too out of place, as she seemed to wear mostly dresses, but... Okay, maybe Turney would be the most out of place.

Either way, it sounded like the office would be going through extensive renovations; paneling, new floors, and even a separate space created for Octavius' office. While Turney didn't know much about these things, he'd assume they'd be out of the office for months.

"When can construction start?" Octavius asked Lilah. "What time frame are we looking at for everything?"

The woman looked at her phone, tapped a few times before looking up, and saying, "As the design has been approved already, I'll get started on the construction documents. They'll be finished over the next few days. Those will then be submitted for permits and contractor bids. The permitting should go smoothly, though. Only taking a few days for approval due to my contacts." She paused, face pinching in thought, before adding, "The start date for construction will depend on the availability of the materials you selected, as well as the schedule of the contractor. If we are lucky, construction could start as early as two weeks. Unlucky, maybe four. Once started, I would say a month to complete due to the small size."

Based on Octavius' frown, he was thinking it was not quick enough for the vampire. To Turney, it sounded reasonable.

"Is there any way to speed up the process? I do understand things take time. Money is, however, not an issue. Contractor wise, go with the best you've worked with, and the one who can start soonest. Let it be known I am willing to double, triple, or more for speed and overtime. I will even pay bonuses for early completion."

The woman was silent for a moment, and she glanced at Scarlett, as if looking for confirmation.

Scarlett, who was sitting on her desk across from them watching, shrugged. "He's over two-thousand-years-old, Lilah. Money truly holds no meaning for him at this point. Octavius could buy every building in this city, and it would not make a dent."

The way she spoke of such vast wealth with such undeniable boredom and disinterest was truly impressive. On another note, if Turney had ever been interested in finding a sugar daddy, Octavius would be the perfect candidate. He wasn't, but damn, did the thought sound appealing right now.

Lilah's eyes widened, but she quickly regained her composure. "Yes, well then. I will contact a few people and let you know what can be done. Some local suppliers will have what we need in terms of building supplies, but may run expensive. Going local will get us what we need faster. The only issue may be some of the custom furniture and fixtures. Some will be antiques, but some things will be made to specification. Let me see what I can do." She grabbed her purse and gathered up the samples off Octavius' desk. "I'll call you later today, after feeling out some things."

"Thank you." Octavius smiled brightly.

Turney watched them exchange a few more pleasantries before she was escorted to the door by Octavius. Once she was gone, Octavius spun around to look at them.

"Exciting, isn't it!?" the vampire exclaimed loudly.

Scarlett scoffed and asked, "How did we go from a spooky theme to the 1920s?"

Octavius got that deer in headlights look that Turney realized primarily appeared when the vampire did not want to answer.

"I suppose I should have expected nothing less than you completely changing your mind after I let you meet her alone," Scarlett drawled, sounding amused.

"I mean, so...it's not entirely my fault. Lilah complimented my clothes, and one thing led to another. Well, the horror, spooky theme sounded less fun the longer we spoke of other things," Octavius finished vaguely.

"Other things..." Scarlett shook her head. "What about the black paper and special printers?"

As he so often did, Octavius waved his hand, as if waving the issue away. "It can be like our special thing." The vampire grew quiet, and his head cocked, lips pursing before suggesting, "Though, maybe we should switch to typewriters? It would fit the theme better."

"Either I get a computer, or you get a new secretary."

Octavius went full pout. "Fine, but I'm getting ones modified to look old!"

Turney found himself smiling as the two continued to bicker like an old married couple. He understood the amount of sighing Scarlett did when dealing with Octavius. The male had a short attention span. And once something popped into his head, if it was anything easy to achieve, it was hard to talk him out of it, if one didn't have the willpower to keep at it.

That being said, the vampire could be rather indecisive at times. No, it was more that Octavius was either indecisive or jumping into doing something without thinking. It was really either-or, and nothing in between. And as much as he jumped into things, the vampire could also change his mind at the drop of a hat.

That being said, Turney found it rather cute how easily excited Octavius was. Along with the way his eyes went wide when he got caught doing something he shouldn't be. The vampire's response was much like a child's, to be honest —denial or pretending he didn't hear you.

Half the time, Octavius' actions left him baffled. The vampire knew he couldn't have solid food. It was not like it would suddenly become not true. Yet, every other day, he had to chase Octavius around the room, trying to stop him from eating something he shouldn't.

Never mind the incident just now with the sucker. Just yesterday, Turney had arrived at work to find Octavius crying as Scarlett scolded him while helping him wash out the ash from his mouth. The goof had taken a bite of the chocolate bar Turney had left on his desk. Octavius' excuse was that he thought there was a chance it wouldn't turn to ash if he let it sit in his mouth and melt. Thinking on it, Turney should probably stop bringing in any sort of solid sweets, unless he planned to eat them right away. Leaving them in his desk, even hiding things, was not working out so well. The vampire probably sniffed them out...

Turney may have found it ridiculously adorable that

Octavius' biggest weakness was not fire, the sun, or even a wooden stake, but his inability to eat solid food—specifically sweets. It sent him into a spiral of 'sad vampire,' who trudged around the office pouting—or more often than not he turned into a sad, mopey bat.

"Everyone, get your coat!" Octavius loudly announced, snapping Turney out of his thoughts.

Having no coat, as it was the middle of summer, Turney didn't move to fetch anything and instead asked, "Where are we going?"

Octavius giggled with obvious glee and rubbed his hands together. "You'll see when we get there!"

Both he and Scarlett let out a sigh at the same time.

Chapter Twelve

Employee Rules

On following the directions Octavius had given him, Turney noticed they were heading towards a rather expensive shopping area, near the Grecian boardwalk. As usual, Octavius was excitedly bouncing in his seat—had been since they'd left the office.

Turney glanced up at the rearview mirror. Behind them trailed a candy apple red Ferrari. Scarlett was too far back to see her through the front window, but he knew it was her. Turney's car only having two seats meant she had to drive herself. Octavius had offered to turn into a bat and sit in the cup holder—Scarlett had declined.

It was almost 8pm now, and most shops were closed, their interior lights off, as were much of the outside ones, besides lamp posts. The area was full of boutiques and specialty shops. Most of the exterior designs were dated like they were straight out of an old movie.

"Stop!" Octavius shouted suddenly.

Turney flinched at the loud yell, instinctively slamming on the breaks, causing both of them to jerk forward hard against their seatbelts and back.

Hands gripping the wheel, he slowly turned to face Octavius, glaring. "Octavius, screaming at your driver is a great way to crash a car."

"Hah..." Octavius smiled weakly and softly stated, "You can park in any of the empty spots right there." The vampire pointed directly to the right.

Good thing Scarlett had been trailing far behind, or she would have crashed into them. Or maybe not. Turney wasn't sure how fast her zombie reflexes were, as she still wouldn't tell him anything about her kind.

He reversed and pulled into the middle diagonal parking spot, in front of what appeared to be the last lit shop in this section of the strip. Scarlett pulled in next to them.

Turney eyed Octavius in concern. The vampire was almost smacking his head into the top of the car with how hard he was bouncing now. Shaking his head, he looked at the lit building. It was two stories, built of dark red brick of multiple shades, and had a black door. There were large display windows on both sides of the door, framed in burnished black. The roof was also black. Above the first floor, there was a wooden jetty that overhung.

The only light came from the large display windows. They were filled with display mannequins wearing what Turney would call fancy clothes, much like Octavius liked to wear. The shop's name was written on the glass in large swooping golden letters.

"*Ageless Antique Threads,*" Turney read hesitantly out loud. "A clothing boutique?" he asked, a sinking suspicion that was more of a screaming one beginning to sink in.

"Not a boutique! Even better, a tailor!" Octavius unbuckled his seatbelt and got out.

"A tailor." Turney sighed to himself before doing the same, locking the car after he closed the door.

He walked over to Octavius. The vampire stood in front of the shop, facing away, waiting for him. Scarlett was already beside the male, eyes empty, neither frowning nor smiling. She looked unimpressed by everything—which was her natural state, so he wasn't sure how she felt about their predicament.

Octavius smiled brightly and did a grand gesture of waving his arms out as he announced, "What better way to match our 1920s office than to dress like we're from the 1920s?"

"Ah..." Turney responded weakly. Yep, a dress code. Man, Turney hated ties.

"You already dress as if you were still in the 1920s," Scarlett pointed out.

Octavius frowned and then reiterated, as if it hadn't been clear the first time. "Well, yes. But we are here for you two, not me. Though I may get a few more outfits while I'm here." His head tilted as his words stopped. The vampire remained silent for a moment, brows pinched, before snapping out of whatever trance he'd been in to brightly say, "Come, come, let's go!"

Octavius wrapped an arm around their shoulders and ushered them inside. Turney went along with much hesitation.

The door let out a soft chime on opening, and a short, stout man with broad shoulders rushed out from behind a thick black curtains. The entry appeared to be a waiting area with red velvet couches. The black curtains must have hidden the rest of the shop.

"Octavius!" the man exclaimed upon spotting them.

"IVAD!" Octavius greeted with a warm smile. Ivad was a gargoyle with impeccable tastes, and had been responsible for his wardrobe for many centuries.

Octavius glanced over at Turney, who was frowning for some reason. But he ignored it and went into introductions.

"Ivad, this is Turney Pimms, my new driver."

Ivad breathed in deeply. His eyebrow rose, but the gargoyle remained polite. "Ah, Mr. Pimms," Ivad rumbled deeply, holding out his hand. "Ivad Barnum. It is a pleasure to meet you."

Turney moved forward and took the other's hand to shake. "Nice to meet you," Turney said politely, before releasing Ivad's hand and stepping back.

Ivad turned to Scarlett. "And, Scarlett, it's been a while, but you are looking as lovely as ever." The gargoyle bowed his head.

Scarlett smiled, responding with a simple nod.

"Now then, down to business. I pulled several bolts after receiving your text message, and made some calls to ensure the necessary time frame. All I need from you two..." The male paused to send smiles toward Turney and Scarlett before continuing, "Is measurements, and the final material selections."

Scarlett spoke up then. "Let me be clear about this. While I don't mind such clothing, I am speaking of the menswear of the time. I'll wear the same as the others up top, and maybe a few bottoms, but I would like some matching skirts, in a style of my choice, to go with them."

Right, the 1920s had never been Scarlett's favorite fashion era for women. She had liked a few specific styles, but none of them would be fitting for working in an office—too flashy.

Ivad frowned, and Octavius found the male looking straight at him. He wasn't sure if the gargoyle was asking for help or for permission. Octavius shrugged and stated, "Do as she asks."

Ivad's shoulders slumped a bit. "Very well, but Rasa will be very disappointed."

"She'll live," Scarlett drawled.

The gargoyle shook his head and beckoned them to follow.

Octavius started to, but Turney softly calling his name stopped him in his tracks. The other two stopped as well, so they collectively turned to stare.

Turney's eyes widened, and he started to fidget where he stood...fists clenching and unclenching. He could hear the human's heartbeat pick up in speed.

Octavius shooed the other two on. "We'll catch up," he assured them, before turning to face Turney and asking, "Yes?"

"How much is this going to cost?"

Octavius blinked in confusion. "Why do you ask?"

Turney's face got that lovely flush it did when the man seemed embarrassed...or upset. The human rubbed the back of his neck before admitting timidly, "I don't think I can afford one outfit here, let alone multiple."

Octavius rolled his eyes—humans and their silly worries. "I'll be paying for it."

"Well, that's one issue solved." Turney cleared his throat. "The other issue would be I have no clue how to clean them."

"I can take care of that easily. Just bring a change of clothes each day. And leave behind what you wore for work, so I can have them cleaned."

His brow rose when Turney's expression shifted from worried to a hesitant smile that looked rather sheepish to Octavius.

"Well, what's wrong now?" Octavius huffed, hands on hips.

"Do...do I have to wear a tie?"

Octavius eyed the human. He supposed the only time the man had worn a tie had been the first day. Turney had messed with it all day long. A rather annoying tidbit he'd forgotten. Something that would drive Octavius crazy if he had to deal with it on a regular basis.

Octavius sighed. "No, you don't."

Turney's smile brightened. "Okay, I'll wear them then!"

Octavius chuckled and led the man through the curtain that the others had disappeared behind.

There was a sitting area with a dark red settee and cream-colored high-backed chairs. In front of that was a circular raised platform and a few dressing rooms. Male and female dress forms were off in the right corner, and Octavius knew the corridor next to them led back into their supply and workroom.

Scarlett was nowhere to be seen, but he figured she was back with the seamstress being measured in private.

Once they entered, Ivad rushed over and dragged

Turney along to stand on the raised platform. Octavius did wonder why it was raised, for Ivad would no doubt have to reach far up to take Turney's upper measurements.

Octavius sat back on the dark red settee and watched. His body felt warm and just filled with happiness. Not literally, of course. His internal temperature rarely changed.

But he was feeling quite pleased with himself. Everything was coming together. He couldn't wait to see them dressed in the 1920s, inside their new 1920s office.

Octavius chuckled when Turney's face reddened as Ivad moved to measure his inseam. He had to admit, Turney was pretty cute—when not lecturing him.

The human also had the sweetest natural scent Octavius had ever come across. He smelled like the perfect buttercream mixed with milk chocolate. Cookie dough! That's what the man smelled like. Octavius had been trying to place the smell for days. Yes, chocolate chip cookie dough. It made him have some rather un-boss-like thoughts.

Octavius was more than curious about how Turney would look in well-fitted clothing. Not that the human looked horrible in the black button-down and black slacks he was wearing. They were just off the rack. So they weren't well fitted to Turney's shape.

Octavius would fully admit he was a bit of a clothing snob. At least, when it came to his own. He would, of course, never mock anyone else for what they were wearing. Well—for the most part.

Turney was handsome. Why take away from that with ill-fitting clothing? And if the human was going to smell like candy, he might as well be a feast for Octavius' eyes.

"All done! I'll be right back," Ivad announced, slapping Turney on the back.

Ivad must have hit too hard as Turney stumbled off the raised platform and to his knees right in front of him. The human's hands came out to grip Octavius' thighs to prevent planting face-first into his crotch.

Turney had a rather nice grip, Octavius mused. Very strong, long fingers, veiny... Octavius' cock twitched in his pants. He quickly pushed the thoughts away, not wanting to go there with his own employee.

Turney stared up at him wide-eyed, a flush spreading across his cheeks. Octavius smirked and glanced down at those strong hands again before saying, "Mind letting go?"

The man looked down, and his hands jerked away, as if he hadn't realized where he'd been grabbing. "Sorry!" Turney's face became even redder. The human hurriedly stood before awkwardly sitting down, scrunched as far away from Octavius as he could on the other end of the settee.

Octavius raised a brow in question. "Relax, I don't bite... much." He giggled at his own joke.

Turney scoffed, but did appear to relax a bit.

They sat there in silence, waiting for Ivad to return. Well, Octavius was waiting. He was sure Turney had no clue what came next.

"We..." Turney started hesitantly before finishing, "Need to talk."

Octavius eyed Turney warily. Nothing good ever came from the phrase 'we need to talk' in his experience.

"About what?"

"So, I understand you are a spontaneous person. Thus, a dress code at the last minute, at night."

"Well, at night really is the only time Ivad can work, him being a gargoyle and all."

Turney opened his mouth, closed it, and then let out a

huge sigh. "You know what...later, explain that later." Turney rubbed his eyes briefly, as if in pain, before continuing. "So anyway, you like to jump into things without explaining or planning, or if there is a plan, you don't usually share it. Not to mention all the information you usually don't share. Which is something we talked about during the last case."

"Yes?" Octavius did remember something along those lines—vaguely.

"I thought it may be best to clarify even more, given your personality."

"If necessary..." Octavius hedged.

"It's very necessary when it comes to new cases. All I'm asking is that a discussion happens, that research happens, and that a plan is clearly outlined before we jump into anything. Don't get me wrong, I'm sure there will be moments that require instant action and there won't be time to plan. But, can we at least try when there is time? More research, more surveillance, fewer surprises?"

Octavius couldn't stop himself from frowning. To be honest, it all sounded so... "But that sounds so boring," he whined.

Turney chuckled. "It may be a little more work, but it will hardly make things boring. All the fun parts of the investigation will still be there, but we'll be more prepared. Please..." Turney met his gaze, his eyes pleading. "For my sanity?"

Only a week and a half on the job, and he already had rules to follow, Octavius thought with a pout. Still, he didn't want to have to find a new driver. And Turney was now his new friend, even if the man didn't know it yet—even if

Turney being human meant it would not be a long friendship...a thought he didn't want to dwell on.

The man fit perfectly into Octavius' life. That Turney hadn't run away screaming was also a plus. Not too many could handle being around him long-term, besides Scarlett. Though he supposed it had been less than two weeks, so that could change. But, Octavius wondered if he could find another driver who smelled like candy!? They didn't grow on trees! He had to do something to make sure his human stuck around!

"Fine, I'll do my best."

"That's all I ask."

A thought occurred. "Since you are going to be more hands-on, maybe I should register you as a detective as well?"

"A detective?"

"It could benefit you. You are a law student."

Turney rubbed his chin, brow pinched. "If I'm remembering correctly, I don't have to be licensed to work as a private detective in the state, as long as I'm working underneath someone who is registered. You are licensed, aren't you...?"

"Of course, I am." Octavius laughed. "I even mentored under a detective in the state...briefly."

"Isn't the state's requirement five years of experience."

Octavius frowned and slowly stated, "I did say briefly."

"Right, the whole vampire thing. Living forever, I suppose five years would be brief to you."

"You would be correct. Apologies, I really am not around humans much. I often forget how vastly different our views on time will be."

Scarlett and Ivad returned then with a young female gargoyle walking behind them who Octavius knew was called Rasa. Scarlett sat down in the plush chair to Octavius' left. The two gargoyles began to show off different fabric selections.

The next hour consisted of going through all the two had pulled. There was a lot that had been pulled. Octavius had managed to narrow it down to fourteen different bolts of fabric in various patterns, materials, and colors. Some were for the undershirt, others the suit. Scarlett picked a few of her own, and Turney remained mostly quiet, besides grunting in agreement when Octavius asked him how he felt about a color or material.

They were going over overcoat material when Octavius' phone rang.

He pulled it out of his trouser pocket, and seeing *Lilah, the architect*, flash across the outer screen, he quickly flipped it open and answered.

"Lilah! So happy to hear from you."

"Mr. Evander, good news. I made some calls. We will be able to start in two days! It will take two weeks to complete construction and get the furniture moved in, but that is mostly due to the crafters needing time to make the specialty pieces."

"Excellent. Why don't we meet up to discuss the details money-wise, and so I can hand over a copy of the keys? I realize it is too late now. But how about tomorrow at the office, around say 5pm?"

"Tomorrow at 5pm would be perfect."

"See you soon."

"Goodbye," she replied.

After hanging up, he happily announced, "Good news! Two weeks paid vacation! Well, not to a specific location or anything, but you don't have to come in and will be paid for it while the office is undergoing construction."

Turney's brows shot up. "Only two weeks? They can finish that fast?"

"Money is a good motivator," Scarlett mused.

"I'm sure it would be even faster if it wasn't for some of the custom furniture, but oh well. Two weeks is perfect as a few of the outfits should be done by then. Right, Ivad?"

"Yes," Ivad responded absently, seeming to be focused on making notes on a small pad of paper.

Octavius' mind ran through all that had happened. Office decoration sorted, outfits sorted, so what was left? Octavius had his driver, but that still left him needing a witch and a tech person. Both would probably be equally hard to find, but for different reasons.

The main issue with finding a witch was more about finding someone who was genuine. Those who truly had magic, and the ability to speak to the dead, generally weren't very open about it. And it was hard to weed through all the frauds to find the ones that were. Octavius had known a few witches over his many years of unlife. Unfortunately, he'd either lost contact with them or they had died. Witches in theory could live forever, but they could still die.

A tech person…now that was more about Octavius' lack of knowledge when it came to modern technology. But also, he just did not know anyone in the field. He could handle a cellphone and simple things, but anything else… Well, he had broken many things.

But maybe, Octavius had someone who could help with that… He eyed Turney.

"Turney, I do have one favor to ask you."

"Yes?" The human met his gaze. Turney's eyes narrowed a bit—suspicious little thing.

"Well, you see, we need someone who understands technology. As you are mostly around the younger generation, could you maybe help me find someone...?" Octavius trailed off, his face feeling hot as a rush of nerves hit him for reasons he couldn't pinpoint as Turney continued to eye him.

The human took in a deep breath. "I suppose I could ask around campus."

Chapter Thirteen

Mr. Sandman, Give Me A Break

Octavius watched in amusement as Turney stumbled off the raised platform, onto his knees in front of him. The human's hands came out to grip Octavius' thighs to prevent planting face-first into his crotch.

Turney peeked up, face flushing beautifully.

Octavius' cock jerked in interest under the human's stare.

"Mind letting go?" Octavius asked smoothly, his mouth twitching as he held back a smirk.

A soft gasp left Turney's lips upon looking down and seeing where his hands were placed, but the man did not let go. Those lovely, veiny hands slid up higher.

Octavius let out a deep chuckle. "Naughty human."

Reaching out with his right hand, he tucked his index finger under Turney's chin, tilting it upward. His fangs descended in hunger, cock hardening at the sight of the human's blood flushed cheeks and heated gaze. A shiver of anticipation ran through him.

Octavius rubbed his thumb over Turney's plush bottom lip. The human's tongue snaked out and brushed against it.

"Since you are down there, why don't you make yourself useful?" Octavius growled thickly.

Turney gulped, drawing his eyes to the veins in the human's neck. That hesitation didn't last long. Octavius' heart skipped along a bit faster, as he watched Turney sink down further—hurriedly freeing Octavius' erection from his trousers.

He frowned—had he forgotten undergarments today? The thought disappeared the second Turney's hands wrapped around his length. The tip of the human's pink tongue probed his slit. Octavius groaned, his prick jerking in Turney's hold.

"Turney," Octavius hissed, hands threading through the man's thick brown hair. The human's tongue circled his head, digging under his foreskin, drawing out a bead of pre-cum. Octavius shuddered as the smell of the human's arousal thickened—an undeniable sweet, musky scent that had Octavius' fangs aching.

Turney's gaze met his. A twinkle of mischief was the only warning he got before the man swallowed him down, taking him fully into his hot, wet mouth, and into the recesses of his throat.

Octavius barked out in pleasure, arching into the heat. But the heat was gone just as quickly, Turney pulling off his cock with an audible pop.

"God, you're big," Turney rasped, licking a wet trail up a vein along the underside of his cock. "Thick too." The human groaned with evident appreciation before swallowing him down again.

One of Turney's devilish hands wrapped around his

base, while the other dropped down to play with Octavius' sensitive balls.

Gasping at the stimulation, his balls rolled in Turney's hold, his cock throbbing, veins bulging as blood pumped through him faster than ever. He struggled not to plunge his hips upward towards Turney's mouth when the human constricted his throat and bobbed up and down. Even in pleasure, his mind screamed to watch his strength, to remain aware of how fragile humans were.

Octavius was near tears, whimpering in need when Turney popped off again.

"I won't break, Octavius," Turney growled huskily. The human grabbed onto his bare hips and yanked him lower, until he was partly off the settee.

Bare? Where the hell did his trousers go? Brain hazy, he gasped as he registered Turney didn't have a single thread on him. Seeing what Turney's ill-fitting clothes had hidden, he decided it was a damn shame clothes were required in society. Broad shoulders, the man had the build of an athlete, defined abs, a happy trail leading to a trimmed patch of brown curls, and a proud cut cock. The human was an impressive size, fully hard, dripping pre-cum, his balls hanging tight to his body.

A firm grip on his cock jerked Octavius' attention away from Turney's body.

"Stop holding back," Turney demanded.

"Turney, my strength."

"Fuck my mouth!"

"I—" Octavius' words cut off on a cry as Turney swallowed him back down without warning, clamping his hand roughly onto Octavius' thighs.

He bucked his hips, hands gripping Turney's hair once

more, and again struggling against his growing need. Turney's hard grip on his thighs felt like a taunt, a dare to move. So, Octavius let go. Grip tightening on Turney's hair, he plunged upward towards the sucking heat.

Turney gagged a bit, before whimpering and whining with need—the human's mouth vibrating around Octavius' shaft. Tears forming in his eyes, Turney met his demand.

"Turney!" Octavius growled as he felt his balls pull closer to his body, his orgasm close.

The need to not be alone in his pleasure was strong, and it urged him to try to seek out the heat of a different hole. But when he tried to push Turney away, the man didn't budge. Octavius found he was locked into place, just taking what Turney gave him.

The constricting heat around him became too much, and helplessly Octavius cried out his release, cock jerking as he spilled his seed down Turney's throat.

OCTAVIUS GASPED, head snapping forward, eyes opening wide while his mind freed itself from the dream.

"Oh no..." He glanced down at the wet spot on his trousers. Well, that explained the no undergarments—and disappearing clothing.

How embarrassing... He hadn't had a wet dream in many centuries. On a sigh, Octavius relaxed in his chair, head leaning against the winged back. By the Gods, had Turney's mouth felt good—his heart skipped a beat.

Oh no—it had felt real—too real. Panic welled up at the implications. Frantically, he reached around for his phone. Not finding it, Octavius jumped from the chair he'd fallen asleep in and sprinted for his room.

Sighing in relief upon spotting the thing on the nightstand next to his canopy bed, he snatched it up and dialed the one number he knew by heart.

He collapsed back on the bed. The minute the line picked up, Octavius blurted out, "I think I projected myself into Turney's dream!"

Scarlett's deep, full-body sigh came over the phone loud and clear. "You think you did?"

"Okay, I definitely did. Or, it could be the Sandman fucking with me again!"

Met the male once, and he'd regretted it ever since! The dreams Octavius had ended up in, just because he had the misfortune of accidentally breaking one of the Sandman's favorite vases.

"You would have smelled him if it was. Since he's an afterthought, I'm going to assume he was not involved."

"Right..."

There was another sigh before she asked, "And you are telling me all this, why?"

"I shared a wet dream with my human driver!" Octavius shrieked hysterically. What was she not understanding?! This was an emergency!

There was silence for a moment, before Scarlett burst out into laughter.

"Scarlett!" Octavius whined.

This was the downfall of having a best friend who found the trials and tribulations of his unlife entertaining, Octavius thought with a sob.

"Give me a moment," she gasped, before once again bursting into laughter.

Octavius huffed, put the phone on speaker mode, and hopped off the bed. Removing his pajama pants and soiled underwear, he marched into his bathroom. He quickly cleaned up and changed into a fresh pair of pants and underwear—all while his friend continued to laugh.

Flopping back onto the bed, he lay there pouting, waiting for the eventual coughing to start, followed by a throat clearing that came after every laughing fit Scarlett ever had.

As he knew she would, Scarlett started to cough and then cleared her throat—her laughter subsiding. "So it was that kind of dream?"

"Yes," Octavius confirmed dryly, as he glared up at the periwinkle drapery over his four-poster canopy bed.

She snickered. "This will certainly make things interesting at the office."

"Scarlett!"

"Well, what do you want me to say?"

"I want my supposed best friend to help me solve this problem!" he snapped.

"Fine, fine. Why can't you just ignore it? It's not like Turney will know, unless you tell him," Scarlett pointed out.

"But that would be so dishonest!"

"Then tell him and let the cards fall where they may. Maybe you'll get laid."

"Scarlett!"

"What do you want me to say, Octavius? You had a wet dream. It was shared, but you had no control over Turney's actions. Yes, you drew both of you there, but your actions in the dream were your own. He didn't do anything he didn't want to. It's not like you did it on purpose. When was the last time you had sex anyway?"

"It's...been a while," Octavius admitted.

It had been a long while, a few hundred years even. Octavius had never been one for meaningless sex with strangers.

"When was the last time you even found yourself interested?"

"Even longer." He winced.

The last time Octavius had just done it to see if he still could. It hadn't been very memorable. And before that...it had been with his last partner, and even that hadn't been the best. Of course, by that time, the relationship had already soured. Octavius' actions had slipped into trying to appease his partner, even if none of it was what he'd wanted, but what he thought he'd had to do to keep the male around.

"So why panic about this? See how he reacts without mentioning it. Go with what feels right. If something happens, it happens."

"But he's my employee..."

"Don't force anything, and let him know saying no won't affect his job."

"But, he's human. What if I start to like him? They are so short-lived." He couldn't help but add softly, "I don't think I'm ready for another relationship."

"Who said anything about a relationship? Why not just have fun? And if you do develop feelings, cross that bridge when it happens." Scarlett huffed. "Honestly, Octavius...I wish you would forget that last asshole you dated. Anytime he comes up, it makes me wish I had killed him. Here's the thing, you are someone who takes so many steps forward, leaps even, without a thought or worry. Don't let one werewolf asshole stop you from leaping forward when it matters most."

TURNEY ARCHED IN BED, eyes still closed. A whine slipped passed his lips as his balls tightened and his cock jerked, spraying cum into his boxer briefs. Prick still twitching, Turney's eyes opened on a breathless gasp, while his mind pulled free of the dream. Licking at his dry lips, a full body shudder overcame him.

Turney huffed in disbelief and wiped the sweat from his brow. It had been hot last night, but the heat he was feeling, and his sweat-covered body, had nothing to do with the actual temperature.

Tossing the covers off, he sat up and stared down at the traitorous wet spot. As the dream flashed through his mind, he flopped back with a groan.

God, it had felt so real. Turney swore he had smelled the male's musk—tasted him on his tongue—as the vampire's face had flooded his brain as he came. It wasn't real, of course, but damn, his imagination had gone wild and had been very...clear.

Thick and long with a ruddy head—not to mention uncut! His hole twitched. Turney wasn't sure how big Octavius really was. But dream Octavius had to be at least eight inches and he could take him however the fuck he wanted. His hole twitched again.

Turney chewed on his bottom lip, seriously debating morality for a split second before muttering, "Fuck it!"

Jumping out of bed, he locked his bedroom door. Turney stripped his dirty boxers off before grabbing lube and the dildo—named the tickle pickle—from his nightstand. Not shaped like a pickle, but the name made him snicker anytime he thought of it—or saw pickles.

Eight inches long, the tickle pickle was over two inches thick, green, realistically shaped with balls and a suction cup. Holding it in his hand, he had to say Octavius' seemed bigger.

Crawling back onto the bed, he tossed the lube and dildo aside to fluff up his pillows. Relaxing back against them, Turney took a calming, shuddered breath—was he really going to do this?

His soft prick twitched as a vision of dream Octavius coming flashed in his mind—yes, yes, he was.

Grabbing the lube, he coated his fingers before shoving the bottle under the pillows. He bent his knees and drew them closer to his body, spreading himself wide. Reaching down, Turney let out a whimper as he prodded his tight pucker—it had been a while. Spreading the lube over the muscle, Turney pushed gently, plunging a finger inside.

He closed his eyes at the sensation, imagining that instead of his fingers it was Octavius'. As he stretched himself open, his spent cock filled again.

"Octavius," Turney moaned. Spearing himself with three fingers, his cries became louder with each brush against his prostate. "Right there!"

But fingers weren't enough to satisfy him. He needed more, and he wanted it to burn—a sweet bite of pain with his pleasure.

On a whimper, Turney pulled his fingers free and blindly reached around his bed for the dildo. Grasping hold of it, he grabbed the bottle from under his pillows and coated the dildo with lube before tossing the bottle aside.

Lining the tip up with his hole, Turney worked it inside himself—whining and grunting at the burning stretch. Enjoying the pain, he plunged it roughly in and out of himself—eyes closed once again. His mind easily conjured up Octavius grinding into him, holding back from giving him the roughness they both wanted.

Then, just as it had been in the dream, it wasn't enough. Whimpering in need, Turney scrambled off the bed onto the hardwood floor. Attaching the sucker to the floor, Turney mounted it, lining the tip up against his hole again before slamming down, crying out as it filled him.

"Yes! Octavius!" Turney cried while he rode the dildo, hard cock bobbing and dripping pre-cum.

Driving himself up and down, he took hold of his cock and started to jerk off frantically. Sweat dripped down his bare body, legs trembling from exertion.

With one last plunge, Turney screamed out while riding his orgasm, cum spurting out, coating his fingers and the floor.

Gasping, he slipped off the dildo and plopped down onto the floor. Turney leaned against the edge of his bed before deciding to just lay right there. Chest heaving, he stared up at the ceiling. Now that it was over, his mind began to rush with instant guilt over what he had just done.

How the hell was he supposed to face Octavius now?!

God, had it felt good...but it was oh so wrong. Yet unfulfilling. Damn, he needed to get laid. Hell, Turney would settle for a backroom bathroom pounding at this point. He just needed something.

Turney sighed. "Focus, Turney. There are other issues besides your lack of sex life," he told himself.

Like the fact he had a wet dream about his boss, and then had proceeded to imagine being fucked by said boss. A boss...who could no doubt smell whenever he was aroused. Turney let out a groan—yep, he was screwed, in a bad way.

Of course, the fact that both had been more satisfying than anything he had experienced during his last few relationships combined was probably something he shouldn't dwell on.

"Focus..."

The only option was to pretend it didn't happen, and quietly make it up to the vampire by...getting him sweet drinks! And finding a tech guy—yes, a tech guy!

But first, a shower...and clean sheets. The floor probably needed a once-over as well.

Chapter Fourteen

Is No One Normal?

Turney flopped, fully showered and dressed, onto his now clean sheets. Running his hands through his damp brown hair, he stared up at his bedroom's white, popcorn textured ceiling.

Sweet drinks could wait. Turney still had a week left to buy things. He had promised Octavius to find or make a watermelon sucker flavored drink. But the best option would probably be to buy a blender and milkshake machine for the office. That way, he could make lots of different things.

Something he'd deal with tomorrow. Today, Turney would focus on solving the bigger issue—the tech person. Or rather, based on what Octavius had said, the vampire needed specifically to find an IT specialist.

Mind running through the people he knew. Not a single person who had vast knowledge of computers, cameras, or anything tech-related came to mind.

He knew if he failed to find someone, Octavius wouldn't be mad. At most, the vampire would pout a bit, and Turney could handle him pouting. Octavius was cute when he pouted.

However, after the dream, and using Octavius'...image in such a way, he felt the need to at least try his best. Besides, he was now a detective in the agency. The vampire had called a few days ago to let Turney know he'd been registered as a detective under Octavius, and that he'd be getting a pay raise.

Turney would still be Octavius' driver, but he would also be officially helping with investigating, instead of just being thrown into the investigation as the vampire's only mode of transportation. So being officially more involved meant it would benefit him if they found someone that could work through any technical issues they had.

Time to go to campus and ask around. On a groan, Turney stood from the bed. Grabbing his car keys from the small pink box on his dresser, he slipped on his shoes. The house was quiet, but that was because his roommate was off on some sort of surfing vacation. Jogging downstairs, he still marveled at how cheap he was renting a room and shared space.

The house was in a nice neighborhood, with two large floors, a finished basement, and a detached three car garage. The outside was burgundy with black trim and wooden accents. The interior was mainly painted in tans, burgundies, and gold. The home could have held at least four other people on top of Turney and Alexander, without having to share a bedroom. For access to most of the house, and a bedroom of his own, Turney was paying the same amount one would pay to stay half a month at a motel.

Alexander owned the house, so he supposed it was due to how nice the guy was, paired with Alexander just not needing the money. Ah...to be rich.

The drive to campus took only five minutes. Since it

made the most sense, Turney started in the computer science department. He came across many of the same answers—no time or no need. Turney supposed when you went to an expensive school, that would ring true for many. Most, but not all, who went here had no money issues.

Turney checked a few other departments with much the same result, though a third option leaked in, of them just not knowing anything about a wide range of technology. Finally, he ended up in his own department, in a last ditch effort to find someone.

Walking down the familiar halls of the *Sterling Law Building*, he found that it wasn't too busy due to it being summer.

Turney turned a corner and slammed into someone very solid. His hands waved in distress as he started to fall back, only to be jerked forward against said solid person he'd run into.

Blinking in shock, Turney looked up and found himself staring at Alexander. "Damn, man. Who knew you were so sturdy under those baggy clothes?" Turney stepped free of his friend's hold and playfully slapped him on the stomach—very firm.

Alexander chuckled at his nonsense. "There is much I hide," the man stated, pausing a few seconds before adding, "under my clothes, that is."

"Apparently. Man, what are you doing here? I thought you'd driven off on a surf trip to places unknown?"

"It was cut short. Short, as in, I never had a chance to leave," Alexander mused brightly, as if not bothered about his ruined trip. Then again, Turney had never seen the man upset about anything. "As for why I'm here, I had some paperwork to fill out." His friend held up a small stack of papers that looked like a whole bunch of forms.

Turney's eyes widened at the papers, wondering how good the man's grip must have been to not have dropped them during their collision.

"Well, that sucks. You'd been talking about the trip for weeks."

"What are you doing here?" Alexander asked, his smile remaining in place.

"Ah, actually, I got a new job at a detective agency and was seeing if anyone who happened to be tech-savvy was looking for a job. To be honest, the agency is very new and disorganized." Realizing that didn't speak well of the place, Turney quickly added, "But the pay is amazing."

Alexander laughed, his smile somehow becoming brighter than before. "You applied for the job on the flyer?"

Turney rubbed the back of his neck. "Ha, yeah..."

"Any luck finding someone?"

"No..." Turney murmured before hesitantly asking, "would you happen to know anyone? Like I said, it pays well, but there are also other benefits!"

Was possible death by meat thirsty wendigos a benefit... not really. But, unlike him, Turney was sure the tech person would get to stay in the office. Besides, all the insane stuff was worth it for the money—right?

There was a large possibility that Turney did not want to be the only human in the office. Having at least one person there who understood how insane shit was would make his freakouts feel less unreasonable.

Alexander hummed happily. "You know, I actually have someone in mind who could need a job in just such an area."

"Wait, really?!" Turney's stomach flipped, and a sense of hope welled up.

Maybe Alexander was his good luck charm! Someone that fate had put into his path to help him right when he was in need—first, a ridiculously affordable place to live, then a job, and now this.

Turney decided at that very moment that it was time for him to move past his distress at Alexander's overly smiley personality and really embrace the man as the good person that he was! Who was he to turn down good fortune!?

"Yes, let me call him. If we are lucky, he may even be on campus."

Turney bounced back and forth on his feet as Alexander called his contact. The person answered right away.

"Cormac, it's me." Alexander laughed at whatever the person said. "Yes, yes, I know. Actually, I was calling because I found a job for you."

Alexander remained silent for a moment before reiterating, "No, not that kind of a job. It's an IT job at an agency. Pays well." The man hummed. "It's worth checking out, trust me. Are you on campus?" He hummed again before adding, "Be at the Life's Liquid Coffee Shop in about five minutes. Bye."

"So, he'll meet us?"

"Yes!"

Turney gave Alexander a quick hug in his excitement. "THANK YOU!"

His friend just smiled and patted him on the back lightly.

LIFE'S LIQUID Coffee Shop was a cute little coffee place a few minutes from campus. It was decorated in earthy tones and a lot of plants. The dark green wooden chairs were surprisingly comfortable. The tables were also wooden, but in a natural stain, with the tops shaped like a leaf.

Turney shifted in his seat nervously, waiting for Cormac. He was alone as his friend had something else he had to do.

According to Alexander, Cormac had recently graduated and was currently working at the helpdesk in the university's tech department. However, Cormac was looking for a better-paying job, and specifically was looking for work as an IT specialist.

It worked well for Turney. And should for Cormac. He doubted that many would be able to find a better entry-level position, and it would be an easy job given the little work that actually happened at the office.

Turney took a sip of his mochaccino and glanced up when the door opened. The man who walked in was tall—probably had at least three inches on him. If this was Cormac, the man was model-like with flawless deep brown skin, a sculpted jawline, striking amber eyes, a thick nose, and plush lips. The guy seemed to have a runner's build, and wore a loose black t-shirt and black jeans. A pair of delicate gold-rimmed glasses perched on the man's nose.

Turney stood up and smiled, holding his hand out when the guy approached his table. "Cormac, right?" he asked hesitantly.

"That would be me," Cormac assured him, voice a bit deep and...growly?

They shook hands, and the man ordered a cup of coffee for himself before taking the seat opposite him.

"So, tell me about the job at the—" Cormac cut off and huffed. "Alexander was vague."

"Well, it is at a detective agency. Very easy work, to be honest. There is a lot of sitting around and getting paid for it, not going to lie. Our boss IS eccentric, but the pay is amazing. It also comes with health benefits. The actual plan, you'll have to talk that over with Octavius. Same with what exactly you will be doing."

"Octavius?" Cormac mused before taking a slow sip from his cup, his eyes meeting Turney's over it.

A shudder ran through him. Why did it feel like he was being stared at by a predator? He got the same feeling when Octavius stared at him too hard.

Shaking the feeling away, he responded. "Octavius is the boss, the main detective, and owner of the agency."

He could have added that he was also a detective. But Turney figured Octavius would just use it as a way to foster paperwork onto him more than anything. And an excuse to endanger his life...

"Ah, so how much exactly is the pay?" Cormac asked, taking another sip.

"Forty-five dollars an hour."

Cormac choked and started to cough. "Forty-five dollars an hour? What's the catch? Low hours?"

"No catch." Besides that paranormal creatures are real, and that their boss was a vampire. "Like I said, Octavius is a bit weird, but the job pays well and has flexible hours, usually at least eight-hour days. There are even free clothes.

Fancy clothes. So, what do you say? Want to come in for an interview?"

Turney straightened in his seat as the man eyed him narrowly, a sharp gaze that put him even more on edge. But Cormac did eventually nod in confirmation.

OH CORMAC, what have you gotten yourself into? Sure, he wanted a better paying job...mostly to buy more games. But it wasn't like he was hurting for funds. His family ensured that would never happen. And if he really wanted more money, all he'd have to do was ask, but he'd be damned if he asked his father for anything. As far as he was concerned, what he did get was solely from his mother.

It seemed stupid to follow some random guy he met through Alexander, of all unfortunate acquaintances. Though forty-five dollars an hour was hard to pass up.

The elevator opened onto the third floor of the multiple-level business building. Turney had eyed him every so often on arriving at the building, looking and smelling slightly guilty, but had said nothing.

It had taken thirty minutes to get to the city of South Windsall from campus. And while the drive had been uneventful and boring enough, for some reason, the closer he had gotten to the place, the more on edge Cormac had felt. The hair on his body stood up further as he walked down the hallway behind Turney.

Man, he didn't even have a resume on him. Shouldn't

they have at least given him time to prepare? How desperate were they, and why?

A scent caught his notice, one that had his instincts on high alert. The urge to flee slammed into him, causing his steps to falter. Warning bells were ringing in his ears, as dread bubbled in his stomach. He forced himself to keep walking, ignoring the warnings, confused at what was going on.

Turney stopped in front of a door that read *The Undead Detective Agency* in fancy lettering. It reminded him of the doors in old mystery movies.

Cormac took a deep breath, and his jaw dropped as the smell that had set him on edge began to overwhelm him, and it finally clicked into place as to why.

But, the why had come too late. The door opened on its own revealing a beautiful...creature. For creature was what it truly was.

"Vampire," Cormac growled.

The beautiful creatures' eyes widened, saying, "Werewolf?"

"What?!" Turney gasped next to him.

Shit, he'd forgotten about the... "Human," Cormac cursed, his gaze snapping towards Turney.

Chapter Fifteen

Natural Enemies

There was construction equipment all around still, and the walls of Octavius' personal office were structurally built but not yet complete. The rest of the office had already been stripped—ready for the new interior paneling and hardwood floors. What little office furniture that had been in the space had been removed.

Octavius eyed the young werewolf, as he took a deep sip from his mug of hot cocoa, before sitting it down on the wheely cart beside him. And the werewolf was indeed young, if the puffed-up chest and posturing was anything to go by. There was a nagging feeling buzzing at the back of his mind that he had met the pup before, but that was preposterous. He knew no werewolf this young.

The youngin eyed him back from his fold-out chair, looking as if he was deciding to attack or not.

Despite their kind's constant squabbles, Octavius had nothing against werewolves. Hell, he had even dated one. It had ended horribly...but he didn't hold a grudge against the entire species.

Out of the corner of his eye, he noticed Turney had

started pacing. "Is no one normal?!" Turney muttered to himself. "Am I surrounded?!"

Octavius tsked—dramatic, as always. The human did look rather good in those sweatpants, though. At least this little confrontation meant he didn't have to deal with the dream from earlier...yet. Yay for distractions.

His glaze slid forward again to the young werewolf, choosing to tune Turney out.

"So, you are good with technology, yes?" Octavius asked with a smile, completely ignoring the tension.

The werewolf continued to stare without saying anything.

Octavius sighed. "Look, young man, this is not a test. It's not a trap. I have no qualms with your species. Why, back in the day, I even dated one of your species. It ended messily, but many relationships do. I'm just looking for someone who is good with technology. I'm old, ancient in fact. Us older paranormals, we need a little help on the tech front. I'm sure you have a few old relatives out there yourself, considering the immortality thing, and you can understand what I'm talking about."

The male took a deep breath and finally spoke. "Yes, I know about technology. I have a Bachelor's degree in Information Technology."

Octavius didn't really know what the degree pertained to, but it was good enough for him. "Excellent. So, you know about computers, cameras, and more?"

"I have some knowledge on cameras. Enough to be of use, I'm sure. Computers should be no issue. I will say, I do also know a little hacking."

"A little," Octavius asked with a brow raised. "You know better than to lie to us old folks, don't you now?"

"Okay, maybe a lot." The werewolf huffed.

Octavius smiled. "Helpful. I would be happy to offer you the job. But first, what is your name. Turney failed to mention it."

"Cormac Laurent."

At the last name, his left eye began to twitch. Surely, he couldn't be... The world was not that small!

"Would you happen to be related to Cléas Laurent?"

Cormac eyed him. "He's my father."

"Of course he is," Octavius let out a harsh laugh.

Of all the werewolves in this state, he had to run into the one related to HIM!

Octavius rubbed his temples, trying to stave off the pain from an oncoming stress headache. "If you accept the offer, I must insist you do not tell him who you work for."

"Why?"

"Because the world is too damn small, and I really don't have any interest in seeing my ex."

Cormac choked on air before gasping out, "The messy breakup!?"

A throat cleared, and Octavius found Turney standing to his right. He guessed the man had tired from pacing. "Yes, Turney?"

"How long ago did you break up?" Turney asked. His tone sounded neutral, but his words had been oddly stiff.

"Does it matter?" Octavius cocked his head. "It's been a few hundred years. Either way, I don't want to see him."

"I mean, after a few hundred years, wouldn't both sides move past it?"

Octavius scoffed at the same time Cormac laughed. He met the werewolf's eyes, and they had a joint understanding at that moment. The definition of a long time really changed the longer you lived.

Shrugging, Octavius faced the human. "Dear Turney, you are again viewing years in the way a human would. For someone of my age, or really any paranormal, two hundred years or more is nothing."

"I'll take the job."

Octavius' head snapped in Cormac's direction. "What?"

"I'll take the job." The male leaned back in his folding chair, a wide smirk plastered on his face.

The smirk wasn't that comforting, to be honest, and had Octavius asking, "Why?"

"Pay is forty-five dollars an hour, right?"

"Yes?"

"And there are health benefits, not that I need them being a werewolf and all."

"Yes, there are..."

"And the schedule is flexible?"

"Correct." Octavius nodded, eyeing the young werewolf suspiciously.

"And it's a chance to piss off my dad."

Octavius sighed—children and their need to anger their parents. "You can't tell him," he reminded.

"I won't," the wolf said, his smile still smug.

"Why are you still smiling?"

"Because my father is a nosy, overbearing bastard who will surely find out on his own without me lifting a finger." Cormac laughed.

Octavius sighed again—that description fit Cléas Laurent perfectly. And the statement alone should have made him say no. But he needed a tech person, and Octavius didn't really feel like looking longer. Or making a new flyer.

Less work would always win out in Octavius' mind. Besides, the idea of pissing off Cléas was sort of appealing.

"Fine, you are hired."

"Perfect. When do I start?"

"Now, but currently the company is on paid leave, while the office is being finished. We are just lucky to have caught them during some downtime so we could meet here."

The wolf glanced around. "I can see that."

"Glad to have you with us, have a nice vacation. It should only be a week. Also, I'll need your information for banking and taxes, and all that stuff."

Cormac nodded. "Can I email it to you?"

"That should be fine. Now..." Octavius eyed the werewolf and tsked at the outfit.

Yet another handsome male who liked to hide under ill-fitting clothes. But it could be fixed! "What are your measurements?"

The wolf blinked. "My...measurements? Measurements of what?"

"Your body measurements," Octavius clarified.

"W-why?"

"No matter, Ivad will take them. Turney, to the tailors!"

Chapter Sixteen

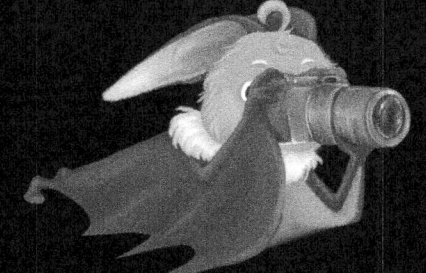

Passing The Time

Octavius fidgeted in his seat for a moment before he forced himself to sit still—for all of a minute. After that, his impatience got the better of him, and he couldn't help but wiggle around, groan, and whine.

"Where is he?!" Octavius huffed, looking through the camera's viewfinder at door 613 at the tackily named motel—The Hole in the Wall.

During his brief years under the private detective that had helped him get his license, Octavius had not learned any sort of patience. He supposed if he hadn't learned any after over two thousand years, he wasn't going to now. It was a rather big flaw, considering how infinite his time was, being a vampire and all.

"Maybe they broke it off?" Turney suggested.

"Highly unlikely. We just saw them flirting yesterday in the office." Sighing, Octavius' hands dropped down, letting the camera rest in his lap.

Sitting in the car was pure agony. Where the hell was Mr. Jonas!? Cheating ass scumbag. The damn man, like clockwork, had checked into The Hole in the Wall motel every Monday, noon on the dot, for the last three months—three months! It was literally in the motel's digital check-in logs.

Of course, it had to be the Monday Octavius was out here that the human had decided to change his damn schedule. It was already 2pm, and Mr. Jonas and his secretary were nowhere in sight. Had Cormac misread the timesheet or something!?

Octavius groaned again—there were so many things he'd rather be doing.

A hand on his leg had him stilling in his seat.

"Relax, Octavius. He'll show. If not, we can always try another day."

Octavius only vaguely heard what Turney said, focusing mainly on the location of the mans hand. Frankly, his mind had dived right into the gutter—so far that an involuntary "mep" left his lips. A sound that he could say he had never made before.

Eyes widening, he met Turney's gaze.

"Um...what was that?" Turney's brows rose, hand releasing his leg.

"It wasn't me!" he snapped, feeling the little blood he was running on surge towards his face.

"Okay, anyway, as I was saying, we can always try again next week."

"But, that's so far away!" Octavius whined, but really he wasn't feeling it at the moment.

It was not a full, genuine whine, and how could it be? One touch and he was feeling as frisky as a rabbit.

At least he knew Turney was not unaffected by the dream they shared. The human did appear to have issues holding his gaze at times. His cheeks were even more prone to flushing than normal. And by the Gods, the random rise in the scent of Turney's arousal seemed to constantly taunt Octavius throughout the day.

However, there had been very little progress in the two and a half weeks since. Which was partly Octavius' fault. He'd been too much of a coward to say anything. And Turney was even more unlikely to bring anything up, as the human didn't know that the dream was anything but a simple dream.

Octavius sighed.

"I get it. This sucks, and it is boring. But not all cases will be as fascinating as wendigos and body parts," Turney hedged.

Ah—Turney thinks his sigh was due to the case...

Octavius sighed even deeper, but decided to just go with it. "Well, yes. I know that. However, I wish the cheaters would at least show up on time for their deviant activities. This scumbag is being such an inconvenience."

Turney chuckled. "Aren't all cheaters an inconvenience? Wasting everyone's time. Their partners. The one they are cheating with. Too much of a coward to do anything except lie and waste everyone's time."

"I understand some have open relationships, with more than one partner and with agreements in place. But I'll never understand cheating by those who willingly enter into a committed monogamous relationship. The minute you realize you no longer want to be with your partner, or rather that your desire to be with others outweighs it, why stay? Why string them along and lie, seeing someone behind their back. There is no hope once you cheat, in my mind. No going back. At least if you are honest about your feelings before you actually go and do it, there is a chance to rekindle."

Turney shrugged. "Some people are just assholes who can't think of anyone else but themselves. Relationships take work. Cheaters are too lazy to put in the work. Once it gets too hard, they look elsewhere. Of course, some just want both the current relationship, the benefits that come with it, and someone on the side."

"Relationships are a lot of work. Especially for paranormals. Long lives and all that. While none of mine have withheld time, I have met those who have been together almost as long as I have been..." Octavius trailed off. He wasn't exactly alive...

"Undead?" Turney offered helpfully.

Octavius chuckled. "Exactly."

Turney crossed his arms. The white linen around his biceps pulled slightly, showing off muscles, which almost made Octavius sigh happily. Turney looked downright edible in his new work clothes. The human was currently wearing a white, peach striped, linen button shirt, with the sleeves unbuttoned at the wrists so he could roll them up to his elbows. Turney was without any sort of jacket—too hot for a human to wear in the current weather. Paired with the shirt was a black tweed waistcoat with matching trousers. It showed off his tapered waist and firm round ass. Octavius just wanted to bite all his buttons off and—

"I can't say I've seen long-lasting relationships. And, obviously, I haven't managed to stay in one myself. But, if my parents were still alive, I would like to think they'd be the perfect example of one."

Octavius pulled his eyes from Turney's body, feeling instantly ashamed at oogling the human during such a conversation. The only saving grace was that Turney had not noticed and was staring blankly out the front window.

He cleared his throat and offered his condolences. "I'm sorry for your loss."

Turney smiled softly. "I only had them for five years, but they were so in love. I could just tell."

Octavius' head cocked. "Five years?"

"Ah, I was adopted." Turney's mouth twisted before adding, "Well, I was in foster care, bouncing around until ten. They were an older couple. Mr. and Mrs. Pimms, both in their early fifties." A small smile appeared on Turney's face. "I was no doubt a handful, but they were so loving. It was hard not to trust them. It was just the three of us. I was alone, and they were as well. No family besides one distant aunt."

"Aunt Trudy?"

Turney chuckled. "Yes, Aunt Trudy. That's who I ended up with after they passed… Drunk driver." Turney's mirth vanished, and the human didn't elaborate further.

Silence reigned. Octavius fidgeted for a few minutes before blurting, "I was the son of a courtesan, and a rich traveling businessman and scholar."

Turney's eyebrow rose at that. "In ancient Rome?"

"Earlier than that. My mother, Efrosyni, resided in the temple of Aphrodite in Ancient Corinth. The women there were…well, to put it plainly, they were servants of the Goddess, but also prostitutes. Well paid and well cared for prostitutes. Highly honored, but still a courtesan. My father, Evandrus, was an unmarried visiting businessman and a scholar. He had several stores set up there already, so when it came about that I was born and was a boy, he did take up residence. He eventually married, but it was to a woman who had been previously divorced due to infertility. I will say his actions fell outside the norm. But his wife, Arete, did become a second mother to me. And despite who my mother was, and that I was a bastard who could not officially be claimed by my father, I was doted on."

"I suppose times were much different then. Did you make his first name your last?"

Octavius nodded. "When it came into fashion and became necessary, yes. I changed it a bit, but essentially the meaning is the same. That aside, I was lucky. I barely felt the stain of my birth, unlike most bastards. I was given freedom that those of my station normally would not have. The right to choose my path. So, instead of becoming a courtesan, I focused on education. I chose the life of a scholar. Mind you, I did still live with my mother at the temple."

"With your looks, I imagine, that decision disappointed many."

Octavius burst into giggles. "Indeed, many were disappointed. I inherited my mother's looks, and my coloring was an oddity. Kissed by Aphrodite, it was claimed. I had many offers, and I could have been quite rich, if I had been interested. But that was my mother's path, not mine. Not that I found shame in it."

"What were your parents like?" Turney asked.

"My mother was very whimsical; a bright woman with strong beliefs in destiny and The Fates. She took pleasure in simple things, and was easy to make happy. Efrosyni claimed the Goddess came to her in a dream and that my birth was a decree of the Goddess herself. She enjoyed her life at the temple and her job. My father was the opposite. More firmly grounded, perhaps a bit stricter, but accepting of my choices. But, I don't know how he would have taken it if I had decided to follow my mother's way of life. They spoiled me. The times were peaceful, which was rare. I admit, I was a bit foolish." Octavius laughed. "I suppose I still am."

Turney chuckled. "I wouldn't say foolish, but maybe a bit silly at times."

He smirked at that. "I'll take silly over foolish."

"When was the last time you saw them?"

"I'm not sure the year, to be honest... It was after the change. Years after, it takes time to get used to everything you see. To become as normal as one can be. I couldn't approach either of them," Octavius stated sadly.

Both his parents lived well into their sixties, shocking considering the time. His father's wife, Arete, had sadly died much earlier. Only a few years after his death had been faked. The rumors he'd heard had crushed him at the time—that she died of a broken heart, due to the loss of a child.

The last time Octavius saw them, they had not been the happy parents he'd remembered. It was one of his regrets, to not have been able to live out a few more years before he could no longer hide that he'd stopped aging. At least, then he could have gone away, said to be traveling—said goodbye. Part of him wondered if he would not have tried to change them, if he had known what he'd eventually come to accept. But, there was no point dwelling on it. In the beginning, he had seen himself as a monster, an abomination. With that mindset, he would have never even considered changing a loved one.

"When we first met, you stated that you weren't changed willingly."

Octavius sighed. "No, I was not. As mentioned, my looks attracted much attention. I turned down many, women and men alike. And my saying no was enough for most. There were always those who wouldn't take no for an answer. But, I was a young and well-trained man who usually could take care of those without help... It didn't work too well when my pursuer was paranormal."

Turney frowned at him. "So, a vampire got angry you said no and turned you for revenge?"

Octavius laughed bitterly as the memories began to surface. "If only it were that simple. Unfortunately, while I ended up a vampire, I was not under the control of one, but something much worse."

His hair stood on end, heart beating a bit faster at the mere thought of the creature. The little blood in his veins was heating in red hot fury, and a touch of fear. The fear was always there. Octavius' vision swam as his temple began to throb.

He blinked and shook his head, trying to drive away the wave of weakness running through his body. It was not so much due to his anger, more his hunger. He'd forgotten to eat that morning. Specifically, he'd not taken the time to consume his weekly intake of blood.

"You don't have to say more if it makes you uncomfortable."

Octavius' eyes widened a touch at the discernable concern in Turney's voice.

"Are you okay? You are looking a bit pale," Turney noted hesitantly.

He must have been in worse shape than he thought. Octavius gave Turney a waned smile. "It's not due to the memories...well, not in part. I will say, I do not wish to discuss this further at the moment. What comes next is not pleasant. But no, my complexion is more due to a lack of blood. I'm afraid I forgot to eat this morning."

The human's eyes widened, and his heartbeat sped up a bit. "So, I'm all alone in a car with a hungry vampire?"

"You are perfectly safe. While I do need to feed each week, I can go without blood for at least a month before becoming a danger to anyone."

Octavius may have been understating his hunger level a bit. He had, as of late, not been taking in the recommended three bags of blood each week. In truth, Octavius had dropped down to just one.

It was no grand scheme to see how little he could survive on. It was more Octavius had become too impatient to take the time to sit down and consume all three bags. And really, he didn't need three bags. He could live on one a week due to his age, as long as he did not forget to eat on the eighth day.

Still, Octavius wasn't at the point he'd attack any unsuspecting human, let alone Turney.

"So, maybe we should head back? You keep blood in the small refrigerator in your office, don't you?" Turney pushed.

"I do, but no, I'm fine."

"Or we could call Scarlett and have her bring you some?"

Yeah, no, that was the last thing he'd do. Scarlett would ask questions as to why forgetting one feeding would weaken him this much. And then Octavius would get into trouble. The lecture he'd get...

"I'm fine, Turney. I can feed when we get back. After we get irrefutable proof of the guy cheating."

"If you are sure..."

"I am." Time for a subject change! "So, your Aunt Trudy."

Turney laughed. "Subtle, Octavius." The human shook

his head. "Aunt Trudy, well, she was an old biddy for sure. And while she did take me in, and I lived in her house until her death about three years ago, I only met her about five times. She paid people to take care of me."

"I'm sorry, that must have been a hard change after your parents."

"It was hard...but..." Turney trailed off, hesitating.

Chapter Seventeen

Got Yah!

Turney hesitated. Considering living with, or rather in, Aunt Trudy's house had led him to his illegal pursuits. He had never really told anyone about that time of his life.

The only ones who knew about his street racing were his fellow street racers. Even then, they had never really known him because Turney kept his face hidden.

Clearing his suddenly dry throat, he just went for it. "It was hard, but the time alone and the freedom let me discover a few hidden talents."

"Your driving?" Octavius' head cocked, something Turney now realized was a habit of his.

"Yes, my driving. I-I got involved with uh—" He gulped and admitted. "Street racing. I had a large allowance, no school besides tutors and the whole home school thing, and I was less grounded than when my parents found me."

"So, the money?"

"While Aunt Trudy did have money, she did not leave it all to me. The bulk went to charity. She left me some, which was surprising due to us not having much of a relationship.

But, definitely not enough to live on for long or enough to pay for Yale. The money was my winnings. That I spun as being money from her. She left me the house and all the possessions in the house, so..."

"So, a locked box full of your money became hers then yours again?"

Turney chuckled. "Yes."

He took a deep breath, staring out the front window, trying to calm his nerves. It wasn't every day you admitted to multiple illegal activities.

"I..." Octavius began softly but trailed off.

Turney glanced over and watched Octavius nibble his plush bottom lip, clearly debating something in his head.

Determination filled the vampire's expression, moments before he blurted, "I accidentally projected myself into your dream."

"You what?"

Octavius began to fidget in his seat, hands balling and un-balling. Wide, innocent eyes stared at him. "Well, you see, it wasn't on purpose. Not that I can't do it on purpose, but that time was not. Not that there was another time before." The vampire's cheeks appeared to regain some color the more he rambled on, not making too much sense after a while.

It didn't take a genius to figure out what dream Octavius was talking about. Only one came to mind, and it had plagued Turney since, in terms of finding himself aroused at awkward moments. As the vampire rambled on, he realized Octavius expected him to be mad about it. Which, when Turney examined how he felt knowing that dream Octavius had actually been real Octavius...well, the emotions were not anger, that's for sure.

Instead, Turney felt heat build with excitement.

"Octavius," he called out, trying to stop the upset the vampire was working himself into—but the rambling kept going.

Turney covered Octavius' mouth. "Octavius, calm down!"

Wide, ocean blue eyes stared at him. He couldn't help but wince when he noticed those beautiful eyes were glossy with unshed tears.

"I'm not mad," Turney huffed, dropping his hand away.

"You're not?" the vampire whispered.

"I'm not."

Octavius shoulders sagged, and he began biting his bottom lip again, peering up at him shyly from under his lashes.

Turney couldn't help but think of the stark contrast between this and the confidence he'd seen in his dream. Both Octavius' shyness now, and his confidence then, were a turn on for sure. His cock was already half hard. And knowing he was not alone in his attraction...

Turney licked his lips, staring hard at the thick bottom lip the vampire was nibbling on.

"Ah, fuck it." He reached out, grabbed the front of Octavius' waist coast, and yanked him forward, slamming his lips against the startled vampire's.

Octavius' mouth parted in a gasp, and Turney took full advantage, delving inside. The vampire tasted sweet on his lips.

His hands threaded through Octavius' blond curls, as he tasted and surveyed the man's mouth. Moments later, Turney found himself shoved back with a lap full of vampire. Octavius let out a low growl before taking over, dominating.

Strong hands threaded through his hair. His cock had hardened completely, and he wished to feel the vampire's hard length grind against his. But pressed so close, there was no room for movement—yet.

While Octavius took his mouth, Turney frantically reached down, trying to find the seat controls. Finding the controls, he lowered and moved the seat back.

Turney groaned, a mixture of relief and pleasure when Octavius ground his hips forward. He tried to give back as good as Octavius gave, but eventually he just gave in to the ravaging, to the demand—to the vampire's control.

His tongue brushed against something sharp. The coppery taste of blood had him pulling free of Octavius' hold.

The taste remained for a moment, and then was gone the next. As if the cut had healed instantly—it was weird.

Breathing heavy, Turney met the vampire's gaze. The eyes meeting his were blown fully black, lips swollen, and fangs descended.

Octavius licked his lips nervously, rasping, "Fangs... Sorry."

Turney's cock throbbed at the admittance and the sight. "Fuck, that's hot."

The vampire's head cocked. With his eyes blown, the way the male was staring made him feel like prey. "Is it now?" A slow grin appeared on Octavius' face.

"Fuck, yes."

Octavius let out the sexist growl Turney had ever heard and attacked his mouth again. Turney whined and whimpered in need. Wrapping his arms around the vampire's neck, he thrust up as Octavius ground his hard, covered length against him.

There was something about the vampire doing it in a three-piece suit that added to how sexy the moment was. At the same time, good God did Turney want to feel his skin. Scratch *want*, he needed it.

Unwinding his right arm from around Octavius' neck, he slid it between them and quickly freed himself from his pants and briefs. His cock was fully hard and shining with pre-cum. Feeling mischievous, instead of freeing Octavius, he gripped the long, hard length through his pants.

Octavius growled and broke the kiss on a hiss, thrusting into Turney's hand. "Gods, your hands are perfect."

Turney chuckled huskily. "Like that, do you?"

"A sin waiting to happen," the vampire hissed, head tossing back on a groan as Turney rubbed Octavius' hard on. "Take me out, Turney."

He happily obliged, freeing Octavius from his slacks and underwear. Turney moaned and licked his lips at first sight of the vampire's large prick. "It's just as big as in the dream."

Long, longer than Turney's, and thicker too. Not to mention uncut. The foreskin was already pulled back, revealing the spongy head. His hole twitched at the thought of it pounding into him. Octavius' cock jerked in his hold, a dollop of pre-cum spurting out.

"By the Gods, your scent just thickened. What naughty thoughts are running through that head?" Octavius groaned.

Turney chuckled. "Only the good kind."

Octavius ground down, his cock rubbing against Turney's, sending them both moaning. Wrapping his hand around them both—though he couldn't come anywhere near close to closing his hand—Turney started to jerk them both off, while they continued to thrust.

The vampire's arms wrapped around his shoulders, Octavius' face burrowing into his neck.

Turney's balls tightened at the soft meows and hisses of pleasure the vampire was letting out. The sounds were driving him to the edge.

Their movements became frantic, rough, the grinding harder. His hand slick with pre-cum, he began to pump faster.

"I want to taste you," Octavius cried out—his words muffled against Turney's neck.

Turney growled. "Do it."

"You don't know what you are saying," the vampire whined.

Oh, but he did. "Bite me, baby. Do it. Take what you need."

There was a loud hiss before sharp pain pierced his neck. The pain was gone instantly, replaced by a pleasure that swept through his entire body.

Turney let out a guttural cry, his release slamming into him as his balls pulled tight and his cock jerked in his hand. The pleasure appeared to double with each pull on his vein.

His cum spurted in ropes over his hand, more and more, before he fell into oversensitivity. Turney's cock softened, but his body was left in ecstasy. Mind floating, he felt almost light-headed.

One last pull on his vein had his body trembling, as did the growl that vibrated against his neck. The hard prick still pressed against his now soft one jerked, Octavius' orgasm mixing with Turney's.

The vampire trembled and shuddered a bit before he felt

Octavius gently extract his fangs from his neck. Pulling back to lean against the steering wheel, Octavius' breath came out in soft puffs.

On the other hand, Turney was gasping for air and trying not to shake apart from what had been the best orgasm he'd ever had.

"Fuck," Turney rasped.

"Fuck, indeed." Octavius giggled.

They sat there in silence while they regained their composure. Octavius looked so gorgeous post-orgasm, with his swollen lips and flush face—flushed with Turney's blood. The thought was heady enough that his prick attempted to perk back to life.

Smirking at his own nonsense, he gave Octavius a lecherous look and brought his cum covered hand before his mouth. Turney gave it a lick without breaking eye contact, humming at the taste.

Octavius let out a masculine chuckle. Turney continued to lick up the slightly bitter mixture of musk, and something unbearably sweet, which he figured must be Octavius' cum. Turney sure as hell didn't remember ever tasting that sweet, or even close to that, in the past. It must have been all the sweet drinks the vampire consumed.

Movement outside had his gaze straying from Octavius. When Turney caught sight of what had drawn his attention, he swore. Grabbing the camera that had been abandoned on the passenger seat, he brought it to his eye.

"Octavius, move!" Turney ordered as he tried to angle the camera around the vampire's body.

While the male quickly moved over to his seat, he was clearly confused. "What, why?" Octavius asked. "What's going on?"

Looking through the viewfinder, he was just in time to see Margery—Mr. Jonas' secretary—exit her car and approach Mr. Jonas, who was waiting right in front of their normal room 613.

"Mr. Jonas is here!"

He heard Octavius gasp.

The couple shamelessly kissed right in front of the door. Turney pressed the button just in time to capture multiple shots of the moment. The sound of the shutter going off broke the tense moment in the car.

"Did you get it?!" Octavius asked in excitement.

Turney took a few more before the couple disappeared inside. "I got it!"

"Yes!" Octavius squealed happily.

He lowered the camera with a relieved sigh and looked at Octavius. The vampire looked back and then started to giggle.

The giggle was just too infectious, and Turney found himself laughing.

As their laughter subsided, Turney suggested, "We should probably get cleaned up...and put away." His gaze roamed to their still exposed cocks.

"I'm afraid not even a shower would hide what we did from Scarlett and Cormac." Octavius tapped his nose. "They will smell it regardless."

"Well, shit. I was more thinking about avoiding public indecency charges. If anyone walked by and saw, well... everything. Not to mention not letting any cum dry on our clothes."

"You have a point," the vampire conceded.

But neither of them moved, and the atmosphere in the car became awkward. Turney's mind began to churn with the fact that he had just slept with his boss... Well, he'd fooled around with his boss. What the hell were they doing?

This was a horrible idea! Of course, the more than horrible idea was them sitting here in the parking lot with their dicks out.

"Shit, Octavius, what now?"

What did either of them want out of this? Hell, Octavius was immortal. What could he even want from someone human? Besides blood, that is.

Octavius cleared his throat. "Well, we can make a big deal out of this, or just accept we are attracted to each other and, like adults, decide what to do about it."

"Do you want a relationship?" Turney asked, hesitantly.

Octavius frowned. "I'm not sure. I don't think I'm ready for a relationship right now. And to be frank, I've been with humans before, but..." The vampire's expression saddened. "They ended as one would expect. Humans don't live long."

Admitting that appeared to make Octavius flinch.

Turney could understand that. "I don't think I could handle growing older as you stayed the same. And no offense, but I don't want to be a vampire."

"None taken. I didn't exactly want to be one either, now, did I?"

"So...where does that leave us?"

Something was urging him to not let things end here. Turney felt he'd have regrets if they never did anything ever again. But, he was in agreement on the relationship part. Turney didn't think he'd be able to handle being in one where he already knew how it ended. And it wasn't just the age part. The idea that he'd leave Octavius all alone one day. Like no, he wasn't in love, but...the possibility was always there, wasn't it? How could he enter into a relationship knowing Octavius would one day have to mourn him? The phrase was: isn't it better to have loved and lost. But why would he want to give someone he loved a new scar? In his mind, it was better to not even start.

Octavius bit his lip. "Maybe we could do that thing youngsters do now. Be friends with goodies?"

Turney frowned. *Friends with goodies*, he repeated in his mind, confused. When the meaning hit him, he burst into laughter. "You mean, friends with benefits!"

Octavius smiled. "Yes, that!"

While part of him was worried he'd get too attached, he couldn't say no. He wanted the vampire in his bed badly. "Let's do it."

"Yeah?" The vampire beamed at him.

Turney nodded. "Yeah."

Chapter Eighteen

The Case Of The Vanishing House

If Cormac sniffed the air one more time, Turney swore he'd find a way to make the werewolf suffer. Like, fuck, he got it. He was literally drenched in Octavius' scent. But dammit, he really didn't need it pointed out after the third fucking time.

Yet, the werewolf kept sniffing the air and laughing under his breath. Scarlett, at least, was just ignoring it. Well, she had appeared a bit excited about it initially.

Personally, the smile she'd sent their way when they returned had been a bit chilling to see on the naturally indifferent and perpetually bored zombie.

Maybe they should have showered. Though, Octavius had claimed it wouldn't have gotten rid of all the smell. But it undoubtedly would have helped. The wet wipes and a visit to a public bathroom had been a quick fix, but not perfect —whatever.

When Cormac once again sniffed the air, throwing a smirk his way, Turney glared. Desk directly across the room from his, the werewolf was sitting there printing photographs —on a regular printer Scarlett had brought in, and Octavius had whined about. All their technical equipment, from cameras to computers, was pretty much new—even if they didn't look it.

Turney's gaze raked over the renovated office. What had once been a completely open space was now three rooms.

The agency's front room—and largest open area—held his, Cormac, and Scarlett's desks. Scarlett being to his right and closest to the door.

The back half of the room had been sectioned off and divided into two. The first of the rooms to the left had become a rather substantial-sized office for Octavius, as well as a meeting area for their team. While the second—the smallest of all the rooms—was turned into an equipment storage area slash full kitchen.

Why had Octavius, a vampire who couldn't eat, added a kitchen? Turney's best guess was that it had to do with him offering to make him sweet drinks. Because it had just been a storage area at the beginning of their first week back, and had somehow become a kitchen by the end of that week.

The laminate floors were replaced with wood. Wood paneling had been added to the walls—it stopped a little bit before the midway point. The other part of the walls were covered in striped dark and light olive green wallpaper. The door was even changed to wooden with frosted glass that had the business name *The Undead Detective Agency* in fancy black letters. Octavius' office door read *Detective Evander*.

Gone were the flimsy chairs and desks. Turney's desk was rectangular, thick, heavy, wooden, and looked antique. Wide legs—very sturdy. Everything most furniture was not nowadays, unless you were willing to spend a fortune. The rest of the desks were similar in style and quality, except for the shape. Octavius and Scarlett had L-shaped desks, while

Cormac's was U-shaped. The meeting table was long and rectangular.

All their desk chairs were those fancy wooden office chairs with wheels. While the underlying structure was wooden, the curled arms, seats, and wingbacks were covered in tufted padded brown leather. They were pretty comfortable to sit in.

The five meeting chairs were smaller, less fancy versions of their desk chairs. The customer chairs in front of Octavius' and Turney's desks were square-shaped and wooden with olive green padded seats and armrests.

There was a little waiting area to the right of the door in the main space, with a tufted brown leather couch, and a random plant that he was pretty sure was fake. Octavius' office had a similar couch as well, along with a few plants.

The disposable office supplies, pens, pencils, etc., were standard. But a few things were definitely throwbacks to the 1920s—like the lamps. Each desk had a lamp with a brass base, and a green glass shade with a pull string. Their computers were....well, they weren't typewriters, at least. They worked as fast and as well as new computers. They just looked like *Windows* computers from the nineties—big and boxy.

The look on Cormac's face when he'd seen the result of him asking for two screens. Turney snorted. The werewolf had gotten two screens all right—two big ass boxy screens. Octavius grudgingly allowed the male to bring in a laptop.

Even after being there for over a week, Turney was still discovering random secrets in the office. He found a secret fridge in one of the wood panels behind his desk—there was also one under Octavius' desk. And while they had file cabinets in Octavius' office, and against the wall near

Turney, they were all basically empty, besides the few human-related cases they'd received.

The one paranormal case they had, that file was hidden in a secret storage room in Octavius' office—hidden seamlessly in the walls. Turney was going to guess the office next door was empty, since the room was big enough that they had to have taken away from the room next door.

All the hidden compartments had been excused away with a wave of Octavius' hand. For if they ever got raided, the vampire claimed. Something about keeping paranormal secrets from the world. Why Octavius thought they may get raided, Turney wasn't exactly sure. He again had to confirm that the vampire had indeed obtained his detective license legally.

Eyes being drawn by movement behind the frosted glass of Octavius' door, his gaze slid over. He couldn't help but smile when he realized what Octavius was doing. While Turney couldn't see him clearly, the vampire was definitely dancing. Probably had his headphones in.

At the sound of the main door bell jingling, Turney glanced away from Octavius' office. The door opened slowly, almost hesitantly, revealing a five foot seven frazzled looking woman who appeared about fifty. Her blue blouse was wrinkled and paired with a pair of mom jeans and white sneakers. The woman's long brunette hair was a mess of frizzy waves, brown eyes wide and fearful. Hands white as snow tightly clutched a small black purse.

Turney remained seated, but Scarlett plastered on a friendly smile and walked from behind her desk to greet the woman.

"Welcome to The Undead Detective Agency. Are you in

need of some assistance?" she asked softly, probably noticing how skittish the woman looked.

"Me... I-I." The woman's lips pinched together, and she audibly gulped. "It will sound crazy. I-it is crazy. I'm... I don't even believe it, and I saw it with my own eyes!"

Turney's brows rose at the slightly high pitch babbling.

"Why don't you come sit down and tell Turney over here what happened while I fetch our lead detective, hm?" Scarlett intoned soothingly. She tried to guide the woman over to one of the chairs in front of his desk, a hand on her back to guide her.

The woman yanked free. "You don't understand! My house disappears!" She waved her hands hysterically. "Just gone! But when it is there...the VOICES! They never shut up!"

At the exact moment of her revelation, the door to Octavius' office burst open. The vampire came out grandly, with his arms spread wide and singing.

"YOU CAN'T—" Octavius cut off, eyes widening as he took in the crying woman and everyone's expressions.

To his credit, he quickly regained composure. Removing his earbuds to store them in his breast pocket, he smoothed his hands down his waistcoat. A brilliant smile, along with sparkling eyes, replaced his shock. "Hello, there. Octavius Evander, at your service. Main detective of the agency. How can we assist you today?"

SCARLETT WALKED in with a tray of mugs, sat two down on Octavius' desk, and handed one to Turney—who sat on the couch by the window. His friend took a seat across the room at the meeting table. Cormac had decided to remain at his desk, saying he'd hear it no matter what room he was in.

Sending a thankful smile Scarlett's way for bringing in hot chocolate, Octavius glanced over to the woman sitting nervously on the other side of his desk—Ms. Savana Holt. It had taken twenty minutes to calm her down enough to get her inside his office.

He supposed calm was not the best word to describe her current frazzled state. Though...now that he thought about it...it was a relatively normal reaction when an uninitiated human came into contact with the paranormal.

Octavius watched her shaking hands wrap around one of the warm cups of hot chocolate and bring it to her lips. She blew on it before taking a sip. Good thing Scarlett hadn't filled it to the top, or there would have been hot chocolate everywhere with how much the cup was trembling in her hands.

"Now then, why don't you tell my associates and me all about your house issues," Octavius encouraged gently, with the friendliest smile he could make.

She sat the cup down, her hands balling together on the desk, tensing again. "Well, I purchased the house, estate really, a few months ago. The owner had passed away or something. I didn't really dig into what happened to the previous owner, to be honest. But it was being sold with everything inside. And I mean everything. All the former owner's belongings remained. They still remain, besides a few things I managed to pack away. And, well, I couldn't pass it up. Some of the furniture are original antiques. The pieces match the plantation style house perfectly. It seemed normal. And a dream buy. I moved to be closer to family, and not only is it close...well... I'm a historical romance author, you see. The setting alone seemed to drip with future inspiration. And it was fine." Savana repeated almost frantically. "It was fine!" But then her shoulders dropped, and she said almost in a whisper, "Until it wasn't."

"Tell us, Ms. Holt, explain what went wrong," Octavius pushed lightly.

She sighed. "I moved in last Monday. The first few days were great. I was exploring, and it was lovely. But, you see, as a writer, I keep odd hours. I have times when my days and nights switch. Such was the case on Wednesday. Wednesday was when things stopped being fine." She bit her lip. "The voices started. Whispering. Horrible, fearful whispering. And the screaming."

Octavius cocked his head. "At what time would you say the voices started?"

"A-around 3am."

Ah...the witching hour. When the power of witches, ghosts, and more were strengthened. Octavius grimaced—it could be any number of nasty things. But his excitement quickly began to build at the thought of going inside a ghost filled, disappearing house. Enough that Octavius had to stop himself from smiling. He didn't think the human would appreciate him smiling, being so distressed and all. But how could he not be excited?! They were about to encounter actual ghosts! He hadn't seen a ghost in years.

"Could you make out what any of the voices were saying?" Scarlett asked, seeming interested in a case for the first time.

"No! Anytime I tried to focus on the words, they turned into a cacophony of screams," she cried.

"What happened after the voices started?" Octavius enquired.

"They wouldn't go away. They just kept coming. Sparse during the daytime and louder at night. And then I began to feel unsafe in the house... There were a few times I tripped and I could have sworn someone was there. That someone had stuck their foot out or pushed me. It became too much by Friday. I couldn't take it anymore. I wasn't sleeping, and I- I felt like I was losing it." She took a calming breath before continuing. "So, I left. I grabbed whatever I could; clothing, anything I deemed too important to leave behind, and got a hotel room."

"Understandable," Octavius soothed. "Not many would stay in such a frightening situation."

She let out a bitter chuckle. "I'm sure you all think I'm crazy. But I'm not. I know what I heard. I know!" she said, almost pleading to be believed, her gaze going around the room to the others.

Octavius reached out and grasped hold of one of her ever-trembling hands. She flinched at his touch, but didn't pull away. He patted her hand before releasing it.

"Breathe, Ms. Holt, we believe you." And he did, for all purposes, her words rang as truth.

Savana's shoulders sagged, and she swallowed, tears forming in her eyes. "There's nowhere else I can go if...if you don't."

"We believe you," Octavius repeated. "Now, tell us what happened after you left."

She cleared her throat. "Well, after I left, I stayed away. But, by Sunday night, I began to feel silly. To doubt what I heard." Savana's shoulders tensed again. "So, I went back. And it was gone!"

"Gone?"

"The house. It had completely vanished! So, of course, I left again, completely freaking out. How can a house just vanish!?" She sobbed, tears falling now. "But then when I went back during the day, it was back! Right where it should be."

"What time did you go there the first time?"

"It was...nearing 4am, I believe. I don't know why I didn't wait until morning, but the urge to prove I imagined things was too strong."

Octavius relaxed back in his chair. "Something certainly is going on in your house. Perhaps even something ghostly. Quite a mystery."

"I honestly feel like I'm going insane. Will you...will you help me?" She sobbed softly. "I can pay whatever you want. I just need my peace back. I need all this to stop!"

While part of him was very empathetic to how terrified the poor woman was, another part was stuck on how excited he was to investigate a ghost-related case. Octavius was doing his best to curb his excitement because, again, smiling happily at a freaked out crying woman would have been severely unprofessional and cruel.

"We will take the case. Fear not, Ms. Holt," Octavius confirmed firmly.

"Thank you!" she gasped, grabbing his hand to shake it. "Thank you!"

Smiling, he pulled his hand free. "Nothing to thank us for. It is what we do. Before I send you with Scarlett to do the paperwork, and perhaps to hand over house keys if you have them, I wish to confirm one thing. You said you felt as if someone were trying to harm you, correct?"

She gnawed on her bottom lip before admitting, "I am a bit clumsy. But there really were moments when, like I said, someone put their foot out to trip me, or that someone pushed me from behind on the steps."

Well, that pretty much confirmed one suspicion... "Then I must ask you to not return to the house until we have found a way to resolve the problem and confirm it is safe. Someone or something is trying to harm you. I must implore you to continue living at the hotel. Or, since you have family close by, you could stay with them."

"Oh, I couldn't possibly stay with family. How would I explain? It's the reason I got a hotel instead of going to them. I-I can stay at the hotel. I brought a few suitcases and my laptop when I left. I can comfortably stay there for some time."

"Perfect. Don't hesitate to call if you remember anything, or if you need anything." Octavius grabbed a business card from the holder on his desk and handed it over.

Savana took it and thanked him again before following Scarlett back out front.

The second the door closed behind the two, Octavius burst from his chair and released his pent-up excitement, jumping around and pumping his fist in the air.

Turney chuckled. "Excited, are you? I have to say, I was impressed with how calm you were during the meeting."

"I'm perfectly capable of controlling my emotions. I'm not a child, you know!" Octavius groused.

"Oh, so you usually just choose not to, is that it?" Turney teased.

"Zip it," Octavius snapped. But, in the end, he shoved his

irritation aside for the task at hand. "Do you not realize what is in Ms. Holt's house!? Ghosts, Turney! Angry ghosts!"

"Are you sure it's ghosts?"

"Well, now that you mention it, ghosts would not be able to make a whole house disappear. So there must be something else involved as well," Octavius mused.

Ghosts could do a lot of scary shit, if they were powerful enough, or controlled by someone who was powerful enough. How powerful they were usually depended on how angry they were. It also depended on what they were a ghost of. Spirits of paranormal creatures tended to be stronger. The spirit of non-undead paranormal creatures that is. Undead paranormals usually could not become ghosts. Either way, a controlled ghost could be set to a specific task, such as scaring people, tripping or pushing. However, they were relatively harmless, due to their lack of physical form.

If Octavius were to bet, he would say a witch was behind this—an evil one.

"Well, let's head off, Turney!" He spun towards the door, intending to leave but was yanked back.

"Oh, no, you don't!" Turney huffed.

"What? What?" Octavius gasped, startled.

"You promised, Octavius. No running off without investigating, or without a plan when paranormals are involved!" Turney thundered.

"But..."

"We are not going near that house until it is properly investigated. At most, I will go there during the day, but only AFTER precautions are taken. No running off!"

"But—" Octavius whined.

"No!"

"Fine!" he hissed.

Chapter Nineteen

Everything Is Better With Glitter

Turney stared blankly as he waited, just as his other coworkers did, for Octavius to call them back to the meeting room.

The vampire had arrived at the office about thirty minutes ago carrying five sizeable brown paper bags and announced that there would be a meeting once he set 'everything' up. Turney was a bit curious about what the 'everything' was.

Octavius had looked just a bit too happy with himself. Which was questionable considering how much he had pouted, whined, and dramatically complained over the last two days about how everything was a waste of time. Yet, the vampire wouldn't let him do any of the research.

Octavius' office door burst open, slamming against the wall, causing Turney to jump.

"Time for the meeting, everyone!" Octavius announced dramatically. "And I mean everyone!" He stared pointedly at Cormac.

Cormac took out his earbuds on a sigh.

Turney's eyes narrowed on the vampire—was that...

glitter in his hair? Standing, he followed the other two in. On entering, he took a seat at the long rectangular meeting table, and his jaw dropped when he caught sight of the giant corkboard to the left of the door.

Holy glitter bomb—literally. The whole board appeared to have a layer of clear glitter on top of it, with colored glitter mixed in to accent some...horrifying pictures. Pins, stickers, and different colored strings linked together in a way he assumed made sense in Octavius' mind.

Cormac snorted at the sight as he sat down at the table, while Scarlett sighed as she so often did. The two had walked around and taken the two chairs against the wall. Turney sat down in one of the free ones across from them, closer to the door.

Octavius stood proudly by his corkboard monstrosity, hands on his hips, a bright, happy smile on his face. He had his glasses on, which Scarlett had confirmed to Turney were fake. It made him wonder if Cormac's were as well—though the werewolf wore his all the time, and not just when he had to read something.

The room was surprisingly clean for how much glitter and construction paper there was on the board. Besides the few random pieces of glitter on the floor and on Octavius, there was nothing to see. How had Octavius hidden the mess? Though he supposed the vampire wasn't exactly a messy individual—perhaps there hadn't been a mess to hide.

"If you would all take one of the books in the center of the table, we can get this meeting started." Octavius waved his hand at the table.

They eyed each other, and then the stack of three brown scrapbooks in the middle of the table, as if it would bite.

Turney had a feeling of what they would find when they opened them up.

"Well?!" the vampire huffed impatiently.

At his insistence, they each grabbed one.

Cormac cleared his throat. "Do I have to be here?"

Octavius glared. "Yes. You may not be going with us tonight, but it is your job to figure out why if we don't return. More so to contact the reapers."

"And you aren't contacting them now. Why?" the werewolf sassed.

"When there is clean-up to be done and we have need of them, they will be contacted."

"Right." Cormac rolled his eyes.

Turney had a feeling that contacting the reapers should not just be for clean-up, and that perhaps what they were about to do would put them in over their heads. But what did he, the dumb human, know?

"I made books for you to follow along as we go through all that has been discovered. Everyone, turn to the first page," Octavius stated proudly.

Oh, this was going to be another glitter explosion. Turney just knew it. Flipping to the first page, he winced… yep, glitter everywhere. It appeared that scrapbooking was what Octavius had decided to go with to make researching fun.

"Excellent," Octavius said when everyone opened to the first page. The vampire grabbed a long wooden pointer from somewhere off the floor. He used it to point to a glittery black and white picture of what could only be described as the definition of an old plantation house. Two stories, columns and all. The image had frowny face tacks pinning it to the board, as well as construction paper frowny emojis around it.

The frowny faces were also around the picture in the scrapbook—with information.

"The house in question is actually a manor built in the 1850s. The Arlget Manor, named so by the first owner, Byran Arlget." He slapped the pointer on a picture of a man in black and white, surrounded by devil emojis before going back to the house. "It was, however, eventually nicknamed Matraquer Manor by the townspeople."

"Bludgeoning Manor...what a promising beginning," Scarlett snarked.

Turney stared down closely at the man's pictures. He suspected based on the degradation of the photograph, that it was probably a copy of a copy. The man's clothes matched the time. Face a swath of sharp angles, frown lines, and haunting eyes. A shudder went down his spine as he looked into them. The man's visage screamed evil. But the feeling didn't survive long under the sheer amount of emojis and glitter. The scrapbook was reminding him of those stories about children finding their parents' work notes and deciding to draw pretty pictures over everything.

"Bludgeoning Manor, huh?" Turney scoffed. "I'm guessing Mr. Arlget was not a good man."

"Yes, not good, for sure. But who knows if Byran was a man at all. Paranormal or not, he was hanged twelve years after the manor was built, for supposedly dozens of murders that involved heavy objects," Octavius mused, as he swung his pointer to an old newspaper clipping copy covered in red glitter, that had some rather graphic depictions of a man that looked like Mr. Arlget...bludgeoning multiple people with various objects. The headline read, *Byran the Bludgeoner Meets Justice*. Turney was going to guess the justice they were referring to was the hanging illustration.

"That could explain the angry ghosts. But not the vanishing house," Scarlett pointed out.

Turney couldn't imagine being angry enough at death to attack innocent people. His mind blanked for a moment at the thought.

He really was just going to calmly accept ghosts were real, wasn't he? Turney couldn't even find it in himself to be shocked at the fact. Though ghosts were a bit easier to believe in than vampires and zombies...

"Yes, we have much more to worry about than ghosts." Octavius nodded. "Ghosts on their own, angry or not, are pretty harmless, due to them not having enough of a physical form. Not that they couldn't end up killing someone with their petty actions. Falling down the stairs wrong can definitely kill any human."

"Is there no history, or rumors of voices, or the house disappearing in the past? Surely, someone would have noticed," Turney wondered.

Octavius tapped the pointer against his legs, bouncing on his feet, before replying, "Nope! It seems all of these issues are only happening now. So, what I believe happened is the second owner, one Ms. Phoebe Koeus, was the reason behind nothing happening." All the strings connecting the house and murders were red. But the one Octavius followed with his pointer now was green, and led to a photograph of a woman with a kind smile and bright eyes surrounded by construction paper flowers. The photo was black and white, and obviously taken near the time of the original owner's. "Not only did she stop it initially, but she was the one who prevented anything from happening all these years. Because owner two is, in fact, also owner three through five." He pointed at another picture surrounded by flowers, except this one had obviously been taken in the last five years.

Wanting a closer look, Turney flipped through some of the pages, past more glittery gore articles about Mr. Arlget, until he found the pictures. Staring hard at the newer one, he found that while her hair was styled differently, and the clothes more modern, it was the same woman. She did not look even a day older, sitting on one of the steps of Arlget Manor. Turney supposed one could assume the similarities were due to being related. But, if one peered closer, it became hard to deny that it was the same person.

"I have a question. First, you called her Ms. Koeus, which suggests she wasn't married, yet she owned a manor in the 1870s? And that was—"

Scarlett cleared her throat. "You are correct. However, lying was the only option when one was a woman and paranormal. Unless you had an actual husband, or a friend willing to fake it, the only other option was to make one up who was always away on business. The other option was to pretend you were a widow."

"Mm, it does mention a husband and her being married, but there are no records of such a husband existing. So, I assumed there never was one," Octavius confirmed. "Putting that aside, it is obvious that owner two through five was a witch!" he announced, waving his hands at his grand reveal.

Cormac, who had remained silent this whole time, choked—more the wolf was trying to smother laugher.

"So, witches are really real?" Turney asked in wonder. "I know you were looking for one, but I suppose I never thought that you were actually looking for a real magic user."

"Yes, very real, though not all magic users are witches," Scarlett drawled. "Witches are real, but not in terms of wands and instant magic. Spells take work, preparation, and most often, the creation of potions. Hexes are also very real. Best advice, never let a witch get a piece of you. There are many things they could do with it, most unpleasant." Scarlett smirked menacingly.

Turney gulped in fear.

"Scarlett, be nice," Octavius said with a frown.

"So..." Turney cleared his throat. "Where is the witch who had been stopping it?"

"Dead." Octavius' head tilted. "It was ruled an accidental death, which led to a distant relative selling the house."

Turney grimaced. "What's the chance of it actually being accidental?"

Octavius chuckled and swung the pointer at a picture on the board behind him without looking. "Zero. How often does one slip in the kitchen, yank a rack of knives down, and have every single one hit?"

Staring at the image the tip of the pointer was on, he cringed. The picture looked to be a crime scene photo. The poor woman's expression was shocked, but there was this feeling of sadness about her. And yeah, the placement of the knives didn't make sense. How could anyone think for a moment that they just landed that way? They were perfectly straight up. Pretty fucking suspicious how they ruled it an accident.

Turney couldn't help but ask, "How could they possibly rule that an accident?"

"It was the most plausible answer," Octavius mused. "No clues to suggest otherwise, besides the placement. But then again, a hex wouldn't leave any behind."

"So, a bad witch murdered our good witch," Turney

rasped. "But then, why didn't the bad witch buy the house? Why let some poor unsuspecting human buy it?"

Scarlett shrugged. "Some just like chaos, but we won't really know until we confront them."

"Confronting them sounds like a horrible idea," Turney pointed out.

As Octavius often did, he waved Turney's worries away. "There are ways to protect ourselves. Do not worry."

How could he not worry? "Does the house actually disappear?" The vampire had yet to clearly state one way or another.

Octavius' brow rose as if it was apparent. "Yes. I had my butler Henry watch it Tuesday night. It vanished at 3am on the dot, and returned exactly one hour later."

Then he guessed their investigation tonight would not be for nothing—joy. "So, tonight…"

"We go into the manor before the clock strikes 3am, and just see what happens."

"That sounds an awful lot like going somewhere and doing something without planning," Turney grumbled.

Octavius huffed. "This is not something one can plan for. What we can do is prepare ourselves!"

The vampire crouched down and then hefted a giant old book onto the table, slamming it open. "Time for a lesson on witches and ghosts!" Octavius giggled.

Oh, boy…

Chapter Twenty

To Horrible Ideas

This was a horrible idea. Would it not have been smarter for Turney to leave this to Scarlett and Octavius?

In fact, Turney being here was pointless, due to the very fact that Scarlett was. She could have driven Octavius. But no, instead of being safe and back at the office with Cormac, he was here about to face an evil witch and ghosts. And he was doing so drenched in sage, armed with some mantras, a necklace, some salt, and a few other questionable items that he was afraid to ask what exactly they were made out of.

The fucked-up part was that while Turney was definitely afraid, a bit of him was excited to see what they would find. Man, he felt like those people who did dangerous shit just for the adrenaline rush. And really, he pretty much was. Because Turney knew that if he said he didn't want to go in, Octavius wouldn't force him. Yet, he remained silent.

Shaking his head on a sigh, Turney turned off his car and eyed his two companions. Octavius was sitting in a cup holder in bat form, while Scarlett took up his passenger seat.

They glanced at him, but they all got out without a word. Turney grabbed the satchel from his trunk, filled with more random shit he couldn't identify, including more sage, and some medical supplies.

Octavius was back in his people form by the time Turney closed the trunk. The silence of the other two, especially Octavius, really drove home that he was not the only one nervous about going inside the house.

"Let's go," Octavius announced, with unusually muted excitement.

Their small group walked up the paved driveway silently. The house was pretty secluded, surrounded by large trees. It looked about the same as in the pictures. There were no lights on inside, from what he could see.

On ascending the steps and reaching the double front doors, Octavius pulled out a set of keys from his pocket. But when the vampire reached out for the door, the left side creaked slowly open before he could even touch it—a light flickering on inside.

"Yep, that's perfectly normal," Turney muttered.

"Well, it is a haunted house, so it kind of is," Octavius pointed out, but it didn't sound as if he believed his own words.

Scarlett, who was on Turney's right, breathed in deeply. "Do you smell that?" she asked, voice sounding...concerned.

Octavius' head cocked, and the vampire took a deep breath in. "I don't smell anything."

Turney would have piped up and said the same, but he didn't smell half the shit they did, so why bother?

"Exactly," Scarlett huffed. "It smells like a brand new house."

Octavius looked at her with a frown. "You are right."

"I have a bad feeling about this." Scarlett crossed her arms. "Perhaps we should come back with reapers instead."

"There is no time. It's ten minutes to three. We have wasted days already." With that bout of stubbornness, Octavius marched inside.

Turney couldn't help but feel that this case was affecting Octavius differently. The vampire's excitement was there, but it was much more contained—filled with uncertainty. Which made Turney extra nervous.

Scarlett sighed and walked past him inside. Not wanting to be left alone, Turney let out a sigh himself and entered.

The inside looked exactly as the pictures showed in the house listing online. Grand foyer and staircase. A small table sat in the middle with a vase full of daisies. The walls were white, the floors a dark hardwood that matched the staircase, trim, and rest of the furniture. Here's hoping the blueprints they had found in the city archives earlier that day were correct.

Turney had wanted to confirm such with Ms. Holt, but she hadn't answered their calls. Probably sleeping—the poor woman had said her hours were off. They had compared them with the listing photographs, so they had some idea of what was where.

A fierce breeze suddenly flowed from behind. Turney flinched inward, heart instantly racing as the front door slammed at his back. They all turned to stare at the door.

"About as creepy as it opening on its own." Turney gulped.

The other two just shrugged.

"Stick together," Octavius ordered firmly.

Yeah, no worries there. Turney had no intention of walking off on his own. He'd seen way too many horror movies to do something that stupid. Rubbing his hand over his chest, he tried to calm his heart.

Turney pulled out the small copy of the blueprints he made. "The best place to start may be the library. Ms. Holt did say the previous owner's belongings came with the house. Only being here a few days, most things should still be where Phoebe Koeus left them."

"As good a place as any," Octavius agreed.

Following Octavius, they headed for a door on the right. According to the prints, it would lead them to a family room that would eventually branch off into the library.

Pushing into the room, they stopped in their tracks at the sight that greeted them.

"Shit," Turney cursed.

The prone figure lying on the coffee table in the center of the room would be hard for anyone to miss. As would the blood. It dripped down, forming a large bloody stain on the beige and blue antique rug.

While Octavius and Scarlett approached, Turney found himself only able to take a single step into the room. One step was enough. The coppery smell of blood hit him, coating his throat. He gagged and flinched back, a flashback of wendigos' many victims filling his mind.

Taking a calming breath through his mouth, he forced himself to examine the body from where he was standing.

It was a woman, and the cause of death was obvious. Hard to miss the knife sticking out of her chest.

"I told her to stay away," Octavius croaked gruffly, rubbing a hand over his face. "That it was too dangerous. Why didn't she listen?"

Turney flinched at the words, realizing he'd avoided looking at the woman's face. He looked then, and had to turn away from what he saw, hand over his mouth. Turney's vision swarmed with tears. His stomach sank and churned. One look was enough, though. Turney doubted he'd ever forget the wide, blank, empty eyes, and the frozen scream of horror on Ms. Holt's face.

No wonder she hadn't been answering... How long had she been here?

Forcing himself to turn back, to stop being a coward, his eyes widened on seeing Octavius reach out for the knife.

"Wait! Should we be touching anything? She was murdered!"

Octavius' eyes were sad when they met his. "Turney, we are past calling the police. No human authority will be investigating her murder. This will have to be dealt with the paranormal way."

"And her family will just never know." Turney rubbed his face. "Just like the families of the wendigos' victims."

He knew why, but even not having a family himself—God, if his parents had just disappeared—at least knowing gave some closure!

"It's for the safety of our world, Turney. I know it may seem harsh and cruel, but humans can't know."

"I know!"

"And if you hadn't been able to handle it, your mind would have been wiped," Scarlett drawled.

"Scarlett!"

"It's the truth, and you know it, Octavius." Her eyes leveled on Turney. "Our world is dangerous. Often, justice is wrought silently. And yes, this world of ours can be harsh and cruel, but so can yours. The fact is, the existence of paranormals cannot be exposed to all of your kind. We would be hunted in mass, experimented on, locked away."

Turney's grimaced, fists balling. He went to speak when the sound of a large grandfather clock chiming silenced his words.

A yelp of surprise slipped out, followed by a grunt when the floor beneath his feet dropped away. Turney heard Scarlett and Octavius startle, but was too busy trying to pick himself up off the floor.

He hadn't fallen far. It was more like the floor had lowered a couple of feet. Groaning, he was thankful when Octavius gripped his upper arm and helped him up.

"Are you alright?" Octavius asked, brows pinched.

Turney winced. "Fine, more unsettled than anything. I'm going to make an educated guess and say the house is no longer where it once was."

Octavius nodded with a frown. "I would say not."

Scarlett calmly walked towards one of the windows and brushed aside the curtains. From where Turney was standing, while he couldn't see outside, it was obviously not night wherever they were.

"This is..." Scarlett's voice trailed off shakily.

Octavius drew a bit closer to her. "What is it? What do you see?"

Scarlett let the curtain fall back into place and turned around. Turney hadn't thought zombies could pale further, but not only was she paler than usual, but her face was drawn in worry and fear. Emotions that seemed out of place on the normally fierce woman.

"It's—"

A loud screech ripped through the air. Turney covered his ears, the sound painful and piercing.

"Shit! It's not ghosts!" Octavius yelled out.

Fear swarmed inside Turney. "What do you mean it's not ghosts!?"

A twisted billowing creature materialized through the floor, mere inches from his face. Turney cried out, arms flailing as he tried to back away.

His screams of terror combined with that of his companions, as freezing cold hands grasped hold of his ankles and dragged him down.

Chapter Twenty-One

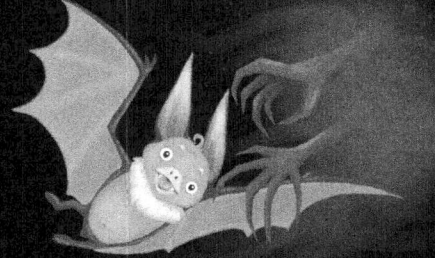

Not A Ghost

Turney landed hard on the wooden floor, his scream was cut off by a grunt of pain. Dragged across the ground by whatever the hell had a hold of him, the satchel slipped free, and the hem of his t-shirt rode up. It made Turney regret convincing Octavius to allow him to wear comfortable clothes tonight.

He did his best to claw at the floor to stop his momentum, but it was no use. After all his kicking and struggling, all Turney had managed to do was flip onto his back. He did get a good look at what had a hold of him—which wasn't a good thing.

Turney's scream of fear could just barely be heard over the creature's shrieking. Body wrapped in billowing rags, the things skin looked leathery, pale gray, and sunken into the bone. The creature's face was a horror show. Shallow cheeks, empty eye sockets, its long white hair flowed around as if blown by an imaginary wind. Worst, its mouth was full of large jagged teeth, always seeming to be open in a silent scream, if not actually screeching. There was an eerie blue and white glow cast over its existence. The creature appeared to flicker, as if not entirely on this plane.

In fear, Turney went back to frantically trying to get away, while the skin of his back, stomach, and sides was rubbed raw as he was dragged over carpet and wood alike.

"Turney!" a familiar voice cried.

Twisted on his stomach, he looked up at the call of his name in time to see Octavius there behind him, reaching out.

The vampire grabbed hold of his hand, stopping his momentum.

Octavius pulled him up into his strong arms, plastering Turney against his hard body. He peered into Octavius' eyes in relief—feeling safe in the vampire's arms.

The male gave him a small smile, but his eyes held a spark of worry.

The worry was warranted. Octavius' eyes widened in shock, while Turney let out an involuntary cry of fear when they tumbled backwards. Loud twin shrieks rang out as they began to once again be dragged away.

Turney clung to Octavius, eyes closed. The sound of doors banging open and closed caused him to flinch.

Octavius hissed loudly. Turney opened his eyes in time to see the vampire slide his right hand along a fully extended fang and fling it out. Blood splattered across the two ghastly monstrosities that had hold of them. They withdrew at the touch of blood, their wails of horror increasing in pitch.

The two creatures began to fly angrily around the room. Coming near, but not daring to get closer—yet.

PULLING TURNEY UP WITH HIM, Octavius smoothed his hands over Turney's hair and began to check him over, looking for injuries. The human was trembling in his arms, staring warily at the wraths.

He brushed a strand of hair out of Turney's face, and maneuvered them so he was between the human and the pissed-off wraths. "Are you alright?"

The terror that had soared through him when he'd seen Turney get dragged away in the opposite direction—Scarlett, he knew would be fine, but Turney...

Turney finally drew his gaze away from the creatures, stepping closer to him. "Besides some nasty rug burns, I think I'm fine. I did lose our bag, though."

Octavius grabbed the hem of Turney's t-shirt and lifted it up. He grimaced at the sight of raw, reddened flesh. Staring, he couldn't help but curse his past self for giving in to Turney's logic that comfortable clothes would be much easier to run in.

Turney spluttered and tried to pull it down. Octavius let him once he'd seen enough. Or more when his thoughts tried to go other places. Such as how Turney's body was a mouthwatering sight, even with the rug burns.

"How about I rub you down with some medical cream once everything is settled?" Octavius' voice came out huskily.

Turney's eyes widened, and his cheeks flushed. "I—"

At that very moment, one of the wraths chose to swoop down and let out an ear-piercing screech right by their faces.

"Shit!" Octavius flinched back, drawing Turney with him.

The poor human was once again trembling, his heart beating rapidly. When another wrath tried to approach again, Octavius hissed at it—rude fucks.

"What are they?" Turney rasped.

"Wraths." He hissed again, as one of the two tried to draw closer.

"Wraths? Are they a kind of ghost?"

"Sort of, but not exactly," Octavius stated. Drawing Turney back with him, one arm around his waist, he took in the room.

They'd been dragged into some sort of study. Since there had been multiple on the blueprints, Octavius wasn't sure where exactly they were. However, there was a medium-sized hole in the far wall between two bookshelves that had not shown in any of the listing photographs—the main reason he'd stopped them.

"So, what are they then?" Turney's question ended in a yelp when both dove towards them.

Bringing his hand up, he once again slid it across a fang, going deeper this time, and flung his blood at the wraths. Their screeches became deafening for a moment before they swirled angrily around and disappeared into the floor.

Turney sagged against Octavius in noticeable relief, before straightening and stepping away. The human grabbed his bleeding hand, brows pulled.

"Will you be alright? That looks deep."

Octavius chuckled. "Not to worry. I heal quick." Pulling

his hand away, he licked the open gash once before dropping his hand by his side. "It will be closed in a minute or two."

"Good."

"Now, to explain wraths. First off, let's get this out of the way. Wraths while yes sounds similar to wraiths, are not the same. Wraith do exist, but are essentially just extremely pissed off ghosts. A generic term for angry ghosts. Wraths on the other hand are the ghost of a specific paranormal species called phantoms."

"Phantoms?"

"Phantoms fall in the undead category of paranormal. Neither living nor dead. Like vampires and zombies, they can be made or born," Scarlett stated as she casually strolled into the room. She was carrying the satchel Turney had said he lost.

"So, they are a ghost of paranormal creatures? Are you alright?" Turney asked.

"I'm fine. And not exactly. While other paranormals can become ghosts, they are considered just that. However, undead paranormals cannot normally become ghosts. Our souls or spirits, if you would, usually pass immediately once we meet our final death. It would be better to say wraths are the captured souls of phantoms. Souls that have been twisted and corrupted to the will of the magic user who murdered them. Wraths have no free will and are impossible for non-magic users to stop without taking down the witch holding them on this plane. It makes them very dangerous."

"There are ways to protect yourself," Octavius rushed to say before admitting, "just not the same way you would if facing a regular human or paranormal ghost."

"Blood hurts them?" Turney asked.

"Paranormal blood will, to a certain degree. Undead blood works best. I would suggest sticking close," Scarlett drawled.

Octavius wasn't exactly sure why their blood helped, but it did. And as they didn't have any other way, it had to do.

Turney sighed. "So, what now? Do we try to leave? Explore the creepy hole in the wall, or maybe just this room?"

Scarlett cleared her throat. "We can't leave. The door won't open, but I imagine that has to do with what I saw outside."

"What did you see?" Octavius inquired. "Nothing good, I surmise."

"A demon box."

"D-demon!?" Turney spluttered.

Octavius' eyes widened—worry filling him at the revelation. "Could you tell what kind?"

"Besides seeing that we are in their plane. Well, a slice of it anyway. I know no more than you do about it."

"What the fuck is a demon box?!" Turney cried.

Looking at the lost human, he grimaced. "It is a trap of sorts. Either a trap set by a demon to capture others, or a trap set to capture a demon."

"It either means a witch being powered by a demon, or one trying to take powers from one. This could get very messy," Scarlett stated dryly.

Messy and dangerous. A witch was one thing, but a demon powered one was a step above. Octavius gnawed on his bottom lip, thinking of what to do. Staying could be deadly—but it wasn't as if they could leave at the moment.

Staring around the room, he took note of the cuckoo clock on the wall. It read ten past three. He hoped that meant time was flowing in sync with the other plane. If so, the house should return at 4am, right?

"As we can't leave yet, we will look around for clues in this room until the house returns to the human plane. Once it has, we will leave and regroup."

Chapter Twenty-Two

A Witch's Diary

Turney began to open various drawers in the antique looking wooden desk, looking for...well, he honestly wasn't sure what he was looking for. Proof of demons? Witches?

He didn't think he'd find much here. All the things Turney had come across, the pens and pencils looked new—just bought and still in packaging. Most likely, the late...

His stomach churned at the memory of the frantic woman who had arrived in their office two days ago. Why had she come back to the house?

"It appears most of the books on the shelf are Ms. Holt's," Scarlett stated, absently flipping through one of the books.

"The books in the boxes are not. I may have found something. I believe these are all—" Octavius waved at the three cardboard boxes on the floor. "—Diaries from the last owner. The last box holds all newer diaries, while the first two are at least a hundred years old. Except for this one." He plucked out one of the small books from the first box.

GET IT TOGETHER

Looking at it, the book was obviously mass-produced and from this decade.

Turney approached and crouched down to examine the contents of the boxes. The boxes themselves weren't very tall, but were long and wide enough to hold three rows of what appeared to be one-inch-thick diaries. Each diary had handwritten dates on the side. The first box had one empty spot right in the first row—where Octavius must have pulled the book from.

Straightening, he examined the book Octavius was holding. The vampire was flipping through it, eyes scanning the pages in a way that made Turney wonder if he was actually able to read at such a fast pace. Scarlett looked to be reading over his shoulder.

Turney frowned. "The one you are holding doesn't have a date on the spine."

Octavius' hand froze on the page he was about to turn. "I believe that is because this was still being written in. This is why it is in the first box. It must have been on the desk, and ended up being the first thing Ms. Holt packed away. Phoebe Koeus is rather vague in her writing," Octavius mused, before going back to flipping through the pages.

Scarlett snorted. "No doubt a habit. The witch trials and burnings made many cautious about writing things down clearly. Even if one were to read, they'd not learn anything paranormal or otherwise."

Turney had a thought. "Isn't it a bit odd that all these things came with the house? Most families auction things off individually, do they not? And her being a witch, wouldn't her family, distant or not, be careful to make sure there was nothing here that would draw any questions?"

Scarlett frowned. "You would be correct. Most families would go through their things and then auction the rest, or have an estate sale. It's possible the distant relatives were not witches, and did not want to put in the time it would take to sell things individually. Or someone wanted things to be found."

Octavius hummed. "I find it surprising that our author wasn't curious enough to go through these diaries. Sure, they are vague, but there's enough here to hold interest, especially that of a historical romance writer. These last entries are certainly vague, but I would think since it had been out..." The vampire frowned. "Well, correct me if I'm wrong, but is it not human nature to want to know someone's last thoughts?"

"What does it say?" Turney asked with interest. Octavius was right, in a way. He, a human, was curious.

"It's dated the day of the Phoebe's death. She titled the last entry *Today, I will tell him.*" The vampire cleared his throat. "*So much time has passed since the first moment our eyes met. It's hard to believe, but the diaries on my shelves bear proof of that. One thought will always remain, plague me, even though you swear it no longer matters. How I wish I could free you. Even if it means you could leave me and never return. No one deserves to live trapped. I know these are words I've said and written hundreds, even thousands of times, but they remain true to this day. Tonight, though, I plan to tell you something that hopefully makes this existence of yours a bit easier. From the time the word love passed both our lips, I hope this moment, the reveal, the result of the combining of our very beings becomes just as precious.*"

Okay—wow. "Yeah, um, I would be reading through those journals from the top. It is a bit weird that Ms. Holt didn't. But also, where is Phoebe's trapped lover?"

Octavius frowned.

Scarlett snorted loudly and rolled her eyes. "Boys...the house is in a demon box."

Octavius' brow rose. "The demon?"

Turney's eyes widened. "But wouldn't that mean the demon was here already? And where is he now? I'd imagine he'd be pretty pissed off at all that has happened?"

"Perhaps, he *was* trapped here already, since the first owner, but was given some sort of freedom by Phoebe, which ended upon her death." Octavius looked down at his watch. "We have twenty minutes left until four. Why don't we grab as many diaries as we can fit into the satchel and head towards the front door?"

That worked for Turney. Who knew if they'd have to fight their way out or not.

They managed to fit about fifteen small journals into his bag. Octavius took over carrying it, saying Turney didn't need anything that would impede his movements.

Leaving the study, they made their way to the front of the house. The wraths had dragged them all the way to the back. As there should have been no room beyond the study, it really made him wonder where the hole went. And then he began to wonder if the dimensions of the room were off, or perhaps all the rooms were off, allowing secret compartments to be built.

Caught up in his thoughts, Turney lagged behind. Noticing he had, he sped up, entering the room where Ms. Holt had met her demise. He went to voice his thoughts but never got a chance.

On entering the room, it was silent for a moment. Octavius and Scarlett were standing in the middle of an empty room—no coffee table or dead body in sight. They were screaming, and must have been the whole time, for when the sound returned, it was as if their words started mid-sentence.

"—Out! Turney, get out! Run!" they screamed in warning.

But it was too late. The floor beneath them turned into a black abyss. The last vision he had before a sharp pain at the back of his head turned everything black was the sight of Octavius trying to get to him.

OCTAVIUS GENTLY PROBED the prominent bump on the back of Turney's head. It wasn't bleeding, but that didn't alleviate his worries. He had seen humans die from less.

As much as he tried, he had failed to reach Turney in time to prevent injury. At least he had been able to grab hold of him before they landed. Octavius wasn't sure the human would have survived the fall.

Pulling Turney into his lap, he looked up, and glared at the woman standing across the room, next to three terrified, bound humans. She was throwing some type of liquid on them.

Her features were too familiar to mistake. Even if she appeared at least fifteen years younger, there was no denying who Octavius was looking at.

"Savana Holt, though I doubt that is your real name."

The witch chuckled, but ignored him to continue with preparations for whatever spell she was working on.

Savana's three twisted souls, the wraths, swirled above her every so often, slamming into the ward around him and his companions. It not only kept the wraths out, but him and Scarlett inside—for now.

The way the witch's form flickered as much as the wraths, made him think perhaps she was not so solidly on this plane at the moment. If he were one to gamble, he would bet that in the course of whatever steps she was taking to steal magic, it had bound her by the rules of the demon box. At least, it had until she completed whatever she was doing.

Octavius also had suspicions that Ms. Holt's plans were not going exactly as she wanted. There had to be a reason she had contacted them.

Either way, Octavius knew he had to put some kind of wards up in the office after this. The witch's spells had too easily bypassed his sense—turning lies into truth.

"Glare all you want, vampire. It won't change that you are stuck in there, while I am out here." Savana's words sounded so sure, haughty even. But now that he was looking for deception, he could tell something was off about them.

Octavius scoffed. "And how long will that remain so?"

"Long enough!" she growled, before returning to whatever she was doing.

Probably long enough for her to accomplish whatever step this was, and to prevent them from stopping her. Sadly, Octavius had an idea of what would happen next. Demon power could be bargained for, paid for, and stolen. Stealing, which no good witch would do, involved blood sacrifices. It could be done with animals, but the more significant the sacrifice, the more power stolen.

Turney groaned, drawing his gaze. Octavius smiled down at him, relieved to see the human's eyes open.

The man blinked, clearly confused as to where he was. Octavius helped him ease into a sitting position with a few words of encouragement.

"There we go. How are you feeling?"

Turney groaned again. "Sore. Head throbbing."

"I imagine it would be."

"What happened?" The man touched the back of his head and winced.

Scarlett, who was sitting, leaning against the stone wall, sighed heavily. "We fell, literally, into her trap."

He watched Turney glance around the room. There wasn't much to see; a wide open space built of stone. There were a few doors, but other than that, really only the wraths, the witch, and her three victims.

"Y-you!? You're alive?" Turney gasped, staring at Savana Holt.

The witch looked up from the large book she was reading and grinned. "Alive and younger. Why don't you come over here, and I can show you what other surprises I have in store?"

Octavius grabbed Turney's hand and pulled him close to his side. Knowing the human would have many questions, he began to whisper, telling Turney of the little he had missed.

"You've only been out a few minutes. It's safe to say we fell into multiple traps this night."

Turney eyed the witch, gaze filling with anger the longer he looked, but soon that was replaced with worry. Octavius realized then that it was becoming easier to understand the young human's emotions.

"Is there nothing we can do to help them?"

"While the ward she has placed protects us from the wraths, it also stops Scarlett and me from leaving it. I'm assuming she did not know Scarlett would come with us. Whatever plan she had in getting our agency involved was screwed up. That being said, she is probably on a time limit for whatever step this is. And too much of a coward to see how her spells will hold up against our precautions."

Because while Savana was taking advantage of a demon box, she was not the one who put it in place. Which meant, her powers did not currently run on demon magic.

Ms. Holt scoffed and picked up a large decorated knife and a wooden bowl. "Coward? I think not! Time crunch perhaps, but you all are nothing compared to me!" She laughed.

Scarlett scoffed.

"Ah, pretty zombie, how would you like to have a new master? Surely, I can make life more interesting?"

Scarlett growled, her face paling, eyes sinking in, shadows under them growing. The lines on her face became harsh and stark for just a moment. "I am no one's property."

The witch hummed. "Pity. How about this, vampire. You give me the human and the zombie, and I'll let you go?"

Turney spluttered, and Scarlett's growling only grew fiercer.

While Octavius knew the offer was not legitimate, the way she spoke seemed natural enough. He had run across this type of creature before. They only considered certain paranormals worthy, while the others were just things to control. An evil witch, who was also a bigot, what a surprise —not.

"Even if the offer was genuine, or proved to be my only way to freedom, I would still not hand my friends over to you. Besides, it has already been established that when the clock strikes four, this ward, and you for that matter, will be gone, until the next witching hour."

Her lips pursed, eyes narrowing, but she said nothing. Just huffed and turned towards the tied-up humans.

Octavius forced himself to look at the humans, meet their eyes, and see their fear. He deserved the memory, to hold this horror that was the result of his own failure so he would not repeat it.

"No!" Turney burst out of his arms and to his feet, lunging towards them.

Octavius jumped up, managing to grab hold of the man in time to stop him from crossing the ward. "Turney, stop!"

"We can't just do nothing!" Turney screamed as he fought against Octavius' hold.

"You will only die trying!"

"Then I die! At least I would have tried!"

As the human continued to fight and scream, wraths slammed against the ward right in front of them, shrieking loudly—daring them to cross.

The witch could barely be seen through the creatures, but it was enough.

"No!" Turney cried as Savana's knife came down. He saw a flash of red in its wake, and the scent of blood filled the room, telling him that it had met its mark.

"Shut him up before I do," the witch yelled.

"Fuck you, bitch! I can't wait for the reapers to torch your ass!" Turney raged.

Holding the struggling man closely, Octavius feared the aftermath of this. He knew he was being selfish—but he couldn't help it. Octavius held Turney's life more precious than that of three strangers.

A stingy wind sliced across his neck at the same time

GET IT TOGETHER

Turney jerked strangely in his hold, his screams becoming a gurgling sound.

"Turney?!" Octavius cried as the man collapsed in his arms, the scent of the human's blood flooding his senses.

Scarlett rushed to his side, helping him lower Turney to the ground.

Octavius let out a cry of horror at the sight of blood gushing out of two large gashes on each side of Turney's neck.

Chapter Twenty-Three

Choices In Worry

Sharp burning pain in his neck, though dulled, pulled Turney awake.

He groaned as he shifted in what must have been the softest bed he'd ever laid on. Too bad it did nothing for his aches.

Turney lay there and took stock of how he was feeling. For one, he was very naked, besides what he was going to assume were bandages wrapped around his stomach. Patches of skin on his stomach, back, and side felt heated, and stung a bit. His head was throbbing, and again there was the odd dull pain in his neck. He remembered sliding through the halls, and hitting his head during the fall. But what the hell happened to his neck?

He went to rub at the pain, but his hand froze when he came into contact with medical wraps. There was also an odd pulling sensation on his right arm.

"What the hell?" Turney eyed the IV attached to his arm. For the first time upon waking up, his gaze swept his surroundings.

From what Turney could tell, he was in a king sized four-poster bed with a periwinkle canopy over it—definitely not a hospital. The canopy's fabric was parted to his right, allowing what appeared to be natural light to shine in on his covered chest. The drapery must have been thick, for no light showed through anywhere else.

The IV line led off into the opening. Reaching out, he grabbed the thick drapery, pulled it back, and found Octavius sitting in a light gray, antique plush chair, fast asleep. The vampire's head was bent forward, chin resting on his chest at the most awkward angle—it looked a bit painful.

The male wasn't dressed to the nines like normal, but instead was in a simple dress shirt and black slacks.

Seeing the vampire, the memories of what he'd been doing right before—whatever had happened—hit him then. Sucking in sharply, he remembered the witch, the humans, the light draining from the first man's eyes.

Jaw clenching, he tried to settle his emotions. There was anger—hatred even—flooding and heating his blood, but also guilt. He just had to figure out where his feelings fell.

At himself? At Octavius? The vampire had held him back. Turney's anger, in that moment, had been mixed. It was there for the witch who was hurting innocents. And for Octavius as well for refusing to release him. But now, he found it was more about how helpless he felt when he'd been unable to do anything to save them.

The talisman on his neck, and the herbs protected him some, but he had no way to fight and protect others. He had assumed Octavius, or even Scarlett, would handle any fight there may be.

Turney couldn't blame Octavius for stopping him. If he hadn't, no doubt there would have been four human sacrifices instead of three. Turney rubbed his eyes and sighed, before looking out at what he could see of the room. A massive window sat behind Octavius, covered by a thin translucent white lace curtain. Thicker periwinkle drapes, similar to the ones around the bed, were tied off on each side. Another chair, like the one the vampire was sitting on, sat near the window, as well as a small table. Beyond that, he couldn't see much besides the hardwood floors, and that the walls appeared to be a light velvet periwinkle.

So, what had happened, and how had he ended up here? Turney was going to assume he was in Octavius' home. The last thing he remembered was searing pain on both sides of his neck, Octavius calling for him, and the vampire's fear filled face. The witch had to have done something, right?

Gazing at the sleeping vampire again, he noted Octavius' brows were pulled together. The vampire was frowning in his sleep—the area below his eyes red and puffy. Had Octavius been crying?

Tossing the thick covers aside, he found the room a bit chilly, but he was naked.

Ignoring the cold, he slipped off the bed, relieved to find that while he wobbled and felt weak, he was able to remain standing. Turney carefully removed the IV line and took a few shuffled steps towards Octavius. He reached out, intending to adjust the placement of the vampire's head, but an elegant hand gripped his before he could.

Octavius' ocean blue eyes felt like they were boring into him. Much like his under eye, they were slightly red around the edges.

The gaze held him in place, and before he gained the courage to speak, Turney found himself pulled into Octavius' arms, the vampire's lips on his.

Turney gasped, which quickly became a moan as Octavius' tongue invaded his mouth.

The kiss was fierce, but brief. Octavius broke it, but their lips remained so close that their breath intermingled.

"I was so afraid you would not wake up." The vampire's voice was a hoarse whisper.

Turney had no chance to respond, for those lips so close to his closed the distance.

Moaning, he wrapped his arms around Octavius' neck, uncaring of his body pains. His cock responded to the vampire's passion.

CUPPING TURNEY'S BARE ASS, Octavius lifted the human into his arms. Taking in his sweet flavor, the underlying fear of the night before drove him forward in desperation—to taste, to savor. The one thought echoing in his head was that he had almost lost him.

His cock thickened in his trousers. Octavius ground his covered prick into Turney's bare ass.

Turney broke the kiss. "God, please, I need that inside me," the human whined.

Octavius chuckled thickly. "Who am I to deny your needs."

Shifting Turney into one arm, he walked over to one of his silver and periwinkle antique dressers, fished inside, and pulled out a small bottle of lube. It had been so long since he'd been interested in sex that Octavius had stopped keeping a bottle in his nightstand by the bed.

He was about to carry the man back to bed when he thought better of it, realizing the dresser was the perfect height for what he needed—just below waist high.

Turney gasped when Octavius hiked him up onto his dresser. His fangs dropped, cock throbbing painfully at the rising scent of Turney's arousal—the human apparently liked being manhandled.

Octavius unbuttoned his slacks and pulled himself free of his underwear. Looking at the beauty before him, Octavius couldn't help but explore. Turney's chest flushed so perfectly—conscious of the man's injuries he made sure he didn't touch the white bandages.

He rubbed his hand over the human's broad chest, shuddering at the little gasps and moans Turney released. The human's rose-colored nipples were hardened, begging to be touched, tasted.

Fangs throbbing, Octavius leaned forwards and sucked on one of Turney's hardened buds, nipping it with one of his fangs before releasing and doing the same to his other. Turney whimpered, arching towards him, crying out in protest when Octavius didn't take what was offered.

A feast is what Turney looked like, even bandaged up. Face flushed, eyes dilated, the man's lips were swollen from their kiss. Needily arching towards him, cock hard and leaking, Turney's balls were nestled up from the way he was sitting. He wanted to see what was hidden underneath.

Letting his claws slip out a bit, Octavius ran them through the trim patch of brown curls around the base of Turney's cock. The man shuddered, gasping at the sensation.

Chuckling thickly, Octavius demanded, "Spread your legs for me, Turney."

Turney let out a needy whine and hurried to do as he asked.

"That's it, darling, show me your pretty hole."

The human had backed himself up on the dresser and pulled his knees up by his head, wrapping his arms under them. The move exposed his puckering hole to Octavius' eyes.

Hissing, his cock jerked at sight. Licking his lips, he dropped to his knees and took Turney's prick into his mouth until his nose bumped against his curls.

"Octavius!" Turney cried.

Sucking a few times, even running a fang along one of the thick veins, Octavius forced himself to release him—he had other plans.

Trailing his tongue down Turney's shaft, he took one of the human's balls into his mouth before dropping further to trail his tongue lower. Turney trembled, whimpering as he left a wet trail over his taint. Mouth hovering over the human's hole.

Turney whined impatiently. "Do something."

"Demanding!" Octavius laughed.

But he gave in, licked at the tight muscle once before probing with his tongue. Turney became more demanding as Octavius opened him up. Each finger he added with lube was not enough for the man. The demands were driving him insane, his cock feeling like he could pop just from the human's need alone.

"Octavius, fuck me! Please!" Turney begged.

"It will burn."

"I don't care! I want it! I need it!"

His balls clenched from where they were trapped in his trousers—fuck. Growling, Octavius surged to his feet, lined up his prick, and pushed inside.

They both cried out in satisfaction, the tight heat around Octavius was glorious. Possibly too tight—but it seemed to be what Turney was craving. It appeared his human liked a little pain with his pleasure. Something he could very much deliver on, Octavius thought smugly.

He snapped his hips forward, giving in to his need and driving into the human's tight hole.

"Oh, God, yes! Fuck me!"

Hissing, he didn't hold back. Pounding into Turney, the human was unable to do much besides take what Octavius was giving him. Putting Turney's legs over his shoulders, Octavius thrust in deeper, folding Turney practically in half so he could capture the man's lips and his moans of pleasure.

The man wrapped his arms around his neck, kissing back as frantically as Octavius' thrusts had become. Feeling his balls pull closer to his body, on the cusp of an orgasm, Octavius released his hold on the man's right leg to reach between them to jerk the human off.

Groaning into Turney's mouth, his cock spurted his release inside the man's tight body. Turney threw his head back on a cry, mouth breaking free of his as he came seconds after Octavius.

Pumping his hips a few more times, Octavius gently pulled free, once he had fully softened. Giving Turney a peck on the lips, he lowered the tired man's legs off his shoulders.

Turney was covered in sweat and breathing heavily. He looked gorgeous in Octavius' eyes.

Giving him one more peck on the lips, Octavius ordered, "Stay here."

Running to the bathroom, he grabbed a cloth and wet it. After cleaning himself up and straightening his clothes, he grabbed another one and returned to Turney. Octavius wiped him free of sweat and other fluids.

Turney flinched at his touch before relaxing a bit.

"Are you in pain?"

"Mm, no. Just not used to someone cleaning me up."

Octavius could only stare, finding it hard to believe.

"Okay, I'm a bit achy, and not just in a pleasant way. Though that is there too."

Gathering his debauched human into his arms, Octavius carried him over to the bed and laid him down.

"I have to say, your past lovers are not measuring up well in my mind." Octavius tossed the dirty cloth in his hamper and tucked Turney in before returning to his seat at the side of the bed.

"What happened?" Turney cleared his throat. The human's cheeks were still flushed from their activities.

"In the chaos, the witch launched a physical attack. The ward protected us from spells and prevented paranormals from crossing, but not normal physical attacks. She threw two blades, and they severed the jugular on both sides of your neck."

Turney blinked, eyes widening.

"The right side was deep enough to cut your inner and outer jugular vein. I managed to slow down the bleeding enough with the help of the coagulant in my saliva, while Scarlett helped pack the cuts with gauze. It worked. And we were able to keep you alive long enough for us to escape and seek medical help at the closest hospital."

"Your saliva... How did you explain the slowed bleeding?"

Truth be, he had to wipe and control a few minds while in 'super vamp' mode, but instead of saying that, he just said, "I can be very persuasive."

"Ah..."

"You still lost a lot of blood."

"How did we escape?" Turney prodded.

"My assumption turned out to be correct. In the process of trying to bind her powers to the demons, she bound herself to the rules of the demon box. Which meant Savana could only complete parts of the spell during the hour the house was in the demon plane," Octavius explained.

Turney frowned. "We saw her dead. Why would she bother doing that? And how did she get her victims if she is so limited?"

"It smelled like death in the room. It's possible the body was real, but had been magically disguised to look like hers. As for why...why does any psychopath do what they do? For personal entertainment? To cause others pain? Who knows?" He shrugged. "I would suggest not trying to rationalize her choices. As for the humans, they may have already been gathered before Savana Holt even stepped foot in our office."

"Why did she even want us there? What was the point?! To see others die?" Turney's face had clouded, his lips pressed in a tight pale line.

"It's not your fault, Turney. If it is any of our faults, it's mine. I should have contacted the reapers."

Which was true. The three humans may have survived if Octavius had contacted them after learning that a witch was involved. Octavius had put his own enjoyment and entertainment over the safety of others—he had put Turney in danger.

"You didn't know how bad it was..."

Octavius sighed and confessed. "Most know that it is not wise to engage a witch without another present. There were other ways we could have learned more about the dangers in the house. Such as entering by daylight. While you forced me to slow down, by researching before we went, there was still more that could have been done."

"If we had taken more time, the three humans would still have been lost," Turney pointed out. "Perhaps more could have been done with the reapers knowing, but what's done is done. There is no bringing back the dead...well, I'm sure there is, but I doubt any of it would be legal."

"No, turning a human into any paranormal without their explicit permission is against our laws. It would be a death sentence to the paranormal who does it."

"Well, then we move forward. Do we know why Savana contacted us in the first place?"

"I imagine sacrificing a vampire would be a big boost to the spell she is casting." Octavius shrugged. "If she had us watched somehow, she would assume correctly that you and I mostly go off on our own. We screwed that up by bringing Scarlett along with us. She was prepared for one paranormal, not two."

"Will it slow her down then in stealing the demon's power?"

"Doubtful. Her involving us was probably due to greed rather than necessity."

"Sounds pretty stupid to me. And arrogant. Why risk everything for a bit more power? What if you had called the reapers?"

"It does seem she knows more about us than she should, doesn't it?"

Octavius would leave that to the reapers to figure out how she knew about his dislike for them.

"Did you bring the journals?" Turney asked.

He nodded. "We have them. Scarlett returned and gathered even more during full daylight. She has been going through them all morning."

"And the reapers?" Turney asked.

"Contacted. They are sending someone tonight. Though the reapers did ask for assistance."

"Then we will read through the journals, gather information, and make sure we are prepared tonight."

Octavius eyed Turney. The human was taking everything well, but missed one thing. Surely, he didn't expect to be allowed near the house again—especially in his condition.

"Turney, there is no *we*."

"What?"

"Correction, there is no *we*, where you would be going. Scarlett and I will return to the house and offer our assistance. You will be staying here."

Turney's face shut down before it twisted, eyes burning with anger. "That's bullshit!"

"Turney, you are injured. You almost died! Please, be reasonable."

"That sure as hell didn't seem to matter when you were fucking me a few minutes ago!"

Octavius growled. "Think as you will, but you will not be going."

"Watch me!" Turney growled back.

He slipped into 'super vamp' mode and reached out.

"Don't you dare," Turney yelped, as he tried to escape the bed.

But Octavius was faster and always would be. He grabbed hold of Turney's arm and reached further metaphysically into the human's mind, overriding his will, pushing him into a deep sleep that would last until tomorrow.

"Bastard," Turney slurred, right before he conked out.

"I'm sorry...but I need you to be safe," Octavius whispered. Leaning over, he kissed Turney's forehead, straightened the covers, and walked away.

Chapter Twenty-Four

Simple Enough!

After making sure Turney was fully under, Octavius made his way through his home to Scarlett.

His friend was in his formal living room, which branched off the foyer. Scarlett was sitting behind the coffee table on the floor. It looked like she had pushed the emerald couch back to give herself more room. She was dressed in a flowery blouse paired with a flowy, burgundy, ankle-length skirt. He wasn't sure if it was the best outfit to fight in, but he wasn't going to risk injury by suggesting she change. Diaries were stacked up on the couch behind her, and there were old books piled around her on the floor.

Scarlett appeared to be going through the current diary in her hand at a human rate. He would say that while they could speed read, they did not always comprehend everything. Slowing down helped them understand details they may have missed or misinterpreted.

Scarlett peered up at him as he entered the room. She took a deep sniff of the air, and her right brow rose. "Nice to know Turney is feeling better."

His cheeks heated. "Hush." Octavius huffed. "I put him back to sleep."

"I'm sure you did," she snickered, wiggling her brows suggestively.

"Not that way!" He pushed some books out of the way with his foot and plopped down onto the floor next to her. "Turney wanted to go with us tonight... I had to make sure he couldn't even if he wanted to."

Scarlett snorted. "Humans can be stubborn and unreasonable."

Octavius frowned. Turney was...stubborn, but he didn't think the man was usually unreasonable. Had Octavius done the right thing? Surely, he had? Turney was in no condition to join such a fight. Turney should have never gone with them in the first place. But, could he have maybe tried harder to explain his reasons?

Octavius winced. Perhaps he could have, but it was done now. Turney would certainly be angry with him when he woke.

Scarlett patted him on the shoulder. "It was for the best. We were asked to assist. To prevent any more loss of life while we wait for whoever the reapers are sending. Bringing Turney would only put another human at risk."

"I know," Octavius sighed. "So, what have you found out?"

"Phoebe Koeus was not the one who trapped the demon there. Which is something we already assumed. For if she had trapped him, she would have been able to easily set him free."

"So, the one who trapped him was, undoubtedly, Byran Arlget," Octavius mused.

Scarlett grunted in confirmation and picked up a large,

frayed green book off the floor, sliding the journal she had been reading out of the way.

The book was old and weathered, the pages crinkling as she flipped it open to a place that was book marked.

"I believe I know what spell was used to trap the demon. Well, perhaps not the exact one, but one close enough that it explains why the demon was not freed, even on the death of the spell's caster."

Octavius leaned over and read the pages Scarlett had opened to. It was, of course, in ancient Latin. It had been so long that it took a moment for Octavius' mind to translate the words.

"The living blood of the caster is needed to break the spell." Convenient, he thought with a snort. "Byran was, of course, hanged far from home."

Scarlett shrugged. "Like I said, it may not be the exact spell. We also don't know what demon was summoned, and this one only mentions the sacrifice of chickens and animals. It does mention that the larger the sacrifice, the greater the power stolen. Either way, it traps the demon in the box along with a small section of the demon plane, and brings wherever the spell was cast into the trapped part of the plane for a set amount of time. The demon cannot enter the home while the house is in the box. During the day, the demon can enter. But they are stuck in an in-between. Like a ghost that can see and wander around, but does not have enough power to do anything."

Well, that explained where the demon currently was. "I bet our bad witch has a few protection wards up, to stop the demon from finding her during the day," he theorized.

"She must, or perhaps she is stuck, but not exactly on the

same plane. We won't really know unless she tells us, to be honest."

"Savana Holt aside...or whoever she is. Phoebe Koeus must have found a way to allow the demon to appear fully on the plane."

Scarlett hummed, reached back, and grabbed an open journal off the couch. "She did, but only at night. Whenever she mentions meeting our mystery demon, it seems to always have been at night. And listen to this..."

DATE: *September 5th, 1923*

I FELL *asleep in his arms last night. I don't know how it happened, or how we went from our constant bickering to feeling so at peace in each other's arms. But, if what we did was against the will of the Gods, then the Gods' will is wrong! Many may question or judge my actions as the gravest sin, or say I was tricked. That sweet words twisted my mind, but I know the truth. Love is what let down my guard. Love is why I allowed him inside me. And beyond any reason, beyond what is believed of his kind, my love was returned.*

OCTAVIUS SHRUGGED, unsure what new information he was supposed to grasp from the passage Scarlett had read out. "We assumed her lover was the demon. This just confirms that."

Scarlett huffed. "Octavius, you missed what I am trying to show you. I thought she was talking about making love in her last entry, but this is many decades before. So that is obviously not what she meant."

"Could it be she found a relative of Byran's to free him?"

"No, she mentioned wanting to free him, not that she could."

He frowned. "Then what do you think Phoebe meant?"

"I believe Phoebe Koeus was pregnant, and that she intended to reveal so the night she died."

Octavius couldn't hold back his gasp. "That...would be rather unfortunate timing. I will say, if she was pregnant, her demon most likely knew already. He'd probably smelled her scent change." He grimaced. "It really just adds reasons for the trapped demon to be enraged, but doesn't really help us."

His head cocked, and a thought occurred to him. "Unless Savana is somehow related to Byran Arlget. Now that I think about it, there is a good chance she is. Who else would know about the demon box, but the family of the one who cast it? Phoebe couldn't free him because she couldn't find any relatives... Or maybe the relatives knowing what he had done, they went into hiding?"

"It's possible." His friend nodded. "Spells are tricky. While the demon was trapped in place, it would not be so easy for an outsider to benefit from it. After all, if the original magic used to cast the spell doesn't mix well with the new witches, there would be backlash. Or it would just not work."

Octavius rubbed his chin. "So, there is a good chance. Perhaps it was one of the reasons she could not risk fighting when she saw that we both came. If she was injured...the demon could break free."

"Perhaps. One may be hesitant to release a demon they plan on stealing magic from. Or one that your relatives trapped. But I wonder if Savana realizes the real reason she should avoid releasing the demon at all cost?" Scarlett drawled.

Octavius nodded. "If she killed his lover and unborn child, the demon's rage would be inconsolable."

An evil smirk slipped onto Scarlett's face. "Why don't we help the demon get a bit of righteous vengeance?"

Catching her meaning, Octavius chuckled. "So, protect any living humans, and stall for time until whoever the reapers send shows up. But while we wait, try to spill a little of her blood and free the demon?"

"Sounds about right." Scarlett shrugged. "Worst comes to worst, we are wrong, and nothing happens. Then the reapers handle it."

"Simple enough!"

Chapter Twenty-Five

Round Two

Simple—ha, what a laugh. Octavius hissed as he slid across the stone floor after getting bitch slapped by one of dozens of wraths flying around.

Shaking his head and pushing past the pain, he jumped up, claws drawn. Coating them in his own blood, Octavius surged forward in another attempt to get to Savana Holt. It wasn't likely to happen, but at least they had already saved the next lot of sacrifices.

Coming early, they had arrived in time to go to the secret passageway through the hole in the wall—the same one they had escaped out of while fleeing the night before. He had to say, the hidden room was unimpressive. All stone, and the main focus was just the stairway down into the underground chamber.

They'd freed six tied-up and terrified humans, and even had time to remove them from the house. They had set them out on the lawn, where Octavius had promptly put them all to sleep so the reapers could deal with the whole missing person issues—memories as well.

So, okay—technically, all of that had been very simple. It was only on returning to the underground that simple had gone out the window.

The clock hit the witching hour to reveal one pissed off, raging witch, and not three wraths but dozens. Three wraths had been a pain to deal with, to begin with. But more than twelve was...

Well, there was no way to do much against them without magic. And while he could make a ward, he wouldn't be able to cross it either. Really, they just had their blood to drive them back. Correction, Octavius had his blood, and Scarlett had a strange pinkish clear liquid. She was an older zombie, and didn't have much of her original blood left, so it mixed with her clear zombie fluids.

Octavius winced in sympathy when Scarlett went flying, slamming hard against the stone wall. He had a mere second to think *that would leave a mark*, before multiple wraths slammed into him and sent him flying back just as she had.

Octavius cried out as his back hit the wall, pain rocking his body. Blood sprayed from his mouth on impact, telling of something rupturing inside. He wasn't exactly sure what was broken, because his whole body was just one large ache at the moment.

"There goes my dinner." Octavius sighed, looking at all the wasted blood now coating the front of his white button-down shirt. He'd dressed down for the occasion, in an off-the-rack undershirt that Scarlett had bought as a gag gift one year and he'd paired it with some black trousers with a small tear at the bottom. No point in ruining another set of fine clothing.

"Surely that is not all you ate," Scarlett drawled, before

taking a moment to growl at a wrath that flew too close to them.

His brows rose as he watched the wrath flee. If this was just one on one, he bet Scarlett would win. One wrath was not scarier than one pissed off zombie Scarlett.

"No, that's not all. You okay?"

She held up her arm, and he grimaced. It was angled the wrong way, and bone was popping through flesh. Scarlett grabbed hold, snapped the bone back, and righted her arm with a small grunt of pain.

Octavius couldn't help but gag. "By the Gods, I hate when you do that." He shuddered.

Scarlett let out a full-body laugh. "I know, but my bones heal rapidly. It will hurt more if I wait."

Octavius was perfectly aware that zombie bones healed faster than almost any other paranormals. So, he did understand doing it, but he also knew she had done it while he was watching because she knew it freaked him out.

"So, why do you think they aren't attacking?" Scarlett asked, staring up at the wraths.

Besides the fact that you are scary? Octavius thought. Not that he would dare say that out loud.

He eyed first the swarm that flew around, blocking the path to the witch, and then Savana, who was looking through an ancient black book, muttering to herself. "I would say it's because we aren't trying to reach Savana. They've most likely been ordered to protect and keep us busy, but not blindly attack."

"I suppose we couldn't just sit and wait until the reapers come?"

Octavius chuckled, but cut the sound off because it hurt too much. "Probably wouldn't look good if we did."

Scarlett stood up with a groan. "Fine, let's get thrown around some more."

Octavius stood up beside her with a very similar moan. "What a way to spend the night."

They charged forward into the thrall. Sadly, they continued to get nowhere in their efforts as they continued to wait for the reapers to show up. Nowhere if you didn't count the extra broken bones and bleeding.

Octavius hissed as a wrath grabbed hold of his obviously broken right leg and dragged him down to the ground. Landing with a pain-filled grunt, his attention was drawn to Scarlett when she let out a shrill cry.

Two wraths had grabbed hold of her ankles and had flown upwards. Hanging upside down, she looked thoroughly shocked at her current predicament, while trying to keep her skirt from moving and exposing her.

Maybe he should have mentioned changing after all, he thought with amusement.

Scarlett must have seen his amused expression, for her shock disappeared, only to be replaced by a glare that was aimed directly at him.

Sending a hesitant smile her way, he quickly averted his eyes. Flinging blood at the wrath that held him, the creature released him, screaming loudly before flying off.

There was so much blood on Octavius that the wraths were actively trying to avoid touching him.

He lay on the ground, trying to not laugh at his friend taking her anger out on the wraths, when suddenly a blinding light blocked his vision.

There was a thud and Scarlett grunted, the wails of the wraths ceased, but he couldn't see anything.

"NO!" he heard Savana Holt cry out just as his vision returned.

The evil witch stood holding her cheek, blood dripping down it, screaming in denial. There was a bloody dagger embedded in the wall behind her.

But all the woman's focus was on the new person standing by the steps. The young woman's face seemed to glow with purity. She had long, straight black hair, beautiful dark eyes, a pert nose, lightly tanned skin, and looked to be of Asian descent. She was wearing a white blouse with a black baby doll-style tank top over it, paired with black jeans and boots.

One thing was clear, the woman was not a reaper. She was a witch—he could smell magic all around her. And she was looking rather unimpressed by Savana's ranting, as the witch attempted to throw spells at her. The bright glow surrounding her seemed to eat away the attacks, blocking whatever came her way.

"Savana Arlget, in the name of the Witch Council, I, Kim Min-ji, hereby charge you with the murder of Phoebe Koeus and three unnamed humans. For your deeds, you have been sentenced to death."

So she changed her last name, but kept her first—how boring.

"You can't do that! I deserve a trial! You—"

Min-ji flicked her hair back behind her. "Who said I planned on doing it myself?" She looked down at what appeared to be perfectly manicured nails. "Why bother getting messy when I don't have to?" she drawled with a sadistic grin.

"What..." Her hand dropped from her cheek, and she

looked down, eyes wide at the blood on her hand. Finally, Savana glanced back at the dagger embedded in the wall behind her. "N-no, you—"

Kim Min-ji clapped her hands together, announcing loudly, "Zor'akos, you are hereby freed!"

"No! What have you done?!" Savana screamed in horror.

An unholy roar drowned out her scream as a large figure burst into existence. The demon stood at least nine feet tall, and wore a black tunic and black pants—no shoes. Muscular, Zor'akos' skin was a purplish-gray color. His claws were white, along with his large bat-like wings. He had a tail, but it was purple with a white tuft at the tip, similar to a lion's. Two giant white horns, shaped identical to that of a ram, came out of the creature's long curly white hair. He had a strong jaw, yet so many of his other features were softer—he would even say the demon was handsome or pretty, if his expression hadn't been twisted with anger.

Octavius wasn't sure if all demons looked so humanoid face-wise. Still, the only thing that showed he was something other was the solid black eyes—no white surrounding them or anything—and his skin.

The demon grabbed hold of the evil witch by the jaw and started to repeatedly slam her against the wall. Zor'akos' inhuman cries of rage barely covered up the sickening crunches or the sound of skin breaking and blood splattering. Savana's screams of pain, though scarcely audible, didn't last long. They quickly changed from screams to gurgles, until finally silence.

While the brutality had not shocked Octavius, witnessing her soul being pulled free of her brutalized remains had. Savana Arlget appeared terrified, even after death. And perhaps she should be terrified. Her soul was covered in filth. Barely any clear light shined through. And then that soul was also grabbed by the demon Zor'akos.

"Your suffering will be tenfold what you have caused on this plane," Zor'akos growled. A dark shadow appeared underneath the dead witch's grimy soul and pulled her downward.

Zor'akos tossed Savana's body across the room with one last roar. The demon remained staring at what was left of the person who took his love away, before drawing back from his rage, and turning to face Kim Min-ji.

"Thank you," the demon said gruffly.

Min-ji nodded. "Your freedom should have never been taken from you. I'm sorry for the hand my people had in it."

Zor'akos' black eyes seemed to fill with grief. "How I wish you had appeared sooner."

"Her line remained in hiding. We would have never located her, if it wasn't for her selfish desire for more power."

Octavius jerked in surprise when a ghostly figure flickered into existence right behind the demon.

Zor'akos spun around, gasping at first sight of the figure. Tears filled the demon's eyes.

Octavius wasn't sure he had ever seen a soul so pure as the woman standing before him. Not a speck of darkness to be seen.

"Phoebe," Zor'akos cried.

"Oh, my love, don't cry. I didn't hide away from wraths or that crazy bitch for weeks, only to part from you again."

The demon's eyes widened. "Y-you...you can't. It wouldn't be right."

"This is my choice."

Zor'akos' face pinched, thoughts clearly warring. But the demon's expression cleared, and he held out his hand.

Instead of taking it, the soul jumped into his hold, wrapping her arms around the demon. As his arms came up to hold her close, the male's tears finally broke free. More shockingly, her bright energy seemed to swell to her center, until it bled to darkness. Her form changed, horns grew from her head, her hands became black-clawed, her face remained just as lovely as before, but her skin had become pure white. Phoebe became...a demon—a happy one at that.

One had to be happy when your other half was smiling down at you, as if you were the only thing in this world that mattered. Their love for each other was clear as a cloudless day. Octavius, for a moment, couldn't help but feel like an interloper, and extremely jealous of what they had. His mind unexpectedly turned to Turney, who was currently sleeping in his bed. Perhaps, a new relationship would not be all bad.

Zor'akos gaze broke from Phoebe's, to meet Octavius. "Thank you. All of you. I am in your debt. My full name is Zor'akosvonatus. Call on me if you ever have need." With that, the two demons disappeared in the blink of an eye, as if they had never been there.

He had witnessed something, and gained knowledge that many would never have. Octavius had seen a soul as pure as its first moment on earth, choosing to dampen its light and become a demon. And then a demon had given his full name, granting him the ability to call on Zor'akos at will, without the need for a true summoning. What a crazy night.

Octavius pushed to a sitting position, mind reeling that he now had the favor of a demon—something that could come in handy, he supposed...

"Now then…" Min-ji approached. "Do you two need any more help?"

Eyeing her, a brilliant idea formed in Octavius' head. He sent Kim Min-ji the brightest smile he could manage while aching so much. "Now that you mention it," he started slyly. "How would you like to become a member of The Undead Detective Agency?"

"The what?"

Chapter Twenty-Six

Now What?

By the time Turney had woken, it had been six in the morning—too late to run out and try to help with anything. So, instead, he had stolen a plush violet robe from Octavius' very luxurious bathroom and wandered around the vampire's house.

Well, he had until he'd run into Henry—last name unknown—Octavius' butler. The man stood a couple of inches shorter than Turney's six feet. He was very well put together, trim, and obviously fit—dressed similar to Octavius. The man had bronzed skin, a sculpted jawline, and sharp features. While he couldn't be sure, Turney thought he may also be a vampire.

Except the male appeared to be in his late forties, possibly even fifties, with white hair at his temples and flowing through his short, thick black hair, and trimmed mustache and beard. The man was a silver fox, to be honest.

Now that Turney thought about it, he didn't really know how the process of becoming a vampire affected one's physical appearance. If one were older, did they de-age?

What about if they were a child when turned? Could they grow older to a certain point before stopping?

Octavius had certainly shown him that everything down below still worked well, whatever his age, Turney thought with a smirk.

Either way, he had followed the man—or vampire—into a living room, right off the foyer, to wait for 'his master'— Henry's words—to return. The room was various shades of emerald, gold accents, and beige.

They had sat in silence for a few minutes before Henry had received a text from Octavius and had run off to grab whatever he'd been instructed to.

So now, Turney waited alone, stuck with his own warring emotions. He was irritated. Irritated that he'd been left behind. Irritated that Octavius had knocked his ass out. But mostly irritated that he had to accept that Octavius was probably right.

He wasn't right about knocking him out, but he was right about it being best that Turney not go. He'd woken up sore— in both a good and awful way—feeling slightly dizzy and unstable on his feet. Hell, Turney had been happy he'd run into Henry after walking around for ten minutes, lost in what must be a mansion. He was not only grateful to not have to wander longer but also to have the help with walking. Henry may have had to half carry him to the living room.

When it came down to it, Turney had been in no condition to fight against even someone who was human, let alone a paranormal creature.

It all made him feel so useless. He was their biggest liability when it came to dangerous cases. Turney just couldn't match any paranormals in strength or abilities. How could he continue his job if he risked hindering his colleagues? Should he keep doing his job, that was a better question.

That aside, there was also the issue of Octavius controlling him, forcing him to sleep. While him being in danger was one thing, him losing his free will was another. He couldn't keep working with the vampire if Octavius thought it was acceptable to take his choices away from him.

Henry walked back into the living room with what looked like two stacks of clothes, a box of medical supplies, and...was that a few bags of blood?

His timing was impeccable. Seconds after the butler separated the stacks of clothes, and laid out the materials on the coffee table, there was the sound of a door opening and closing—followed by shuffling of uneven footsteps.

Henry straightened and faced the opposite opening to the one he used—the one he'd claimed led to the front foyer and main front door.

The shuffling grew louder, and soon Scarlett and Octavius appeared.

Turney's eyes widened as he took the two in. At the same time, Henry gasped in horror. "Master!"

Henry rushed to their sides. Turney followed at a slower pace. A touch of worry filled him as he stared at the two.

Both appeared worse for wear. Clothes torn and bloody. Correction, Octavius was bloody. Scarlett, while clearly injured, had little in the way of blood on her. Instead there was some weird clear liquid that was a touch pink. Her smaller form did appear to be standing straight, at least. On the other hand, Octavius looked as if someone had sprayed blood on him, and he was leaning heavily against the zombie. Something was wrong with his right leg.

The sight was worrying. Turney felt a need to pick him up to lessen his pain, but he wasn't sure how or where to grab hold of him. Instead, he helped Henry guide the two over to the couches and chairs.

Getting Scarlett settled on the couch and Octavius into a plush chair, he sat across from the vampire. Henry tried to flutter around Octavius, but was quickly waved away to care for Scarlett.

Injuries aside, Scarlett seemed bored, and you wouldn't realize she was in pain if it wasn't for the winces that twisted her face when she moved. The bright smile on Octavius' face was comforting, yet not at the same time. The sight of the vampire's smile had started to ease his worries, until he noticed the dried blood on Octavius' mouth and chin—making the smile look all sorts of fucked up.

The one thing this display did was confirm just how dangerous it would have been if he'd gone with them. Because if this was how an ancient vampire and a zombie—age unknown—fared, how would a human?

"You look awful," Turney blurted, hands bunching in his lap. "Are you okay?"

Octavius waved his hand. "I'll heal." His smile widened as if to back up his words. Unfortunately, blood chose that moment to drip down the corner of his mouth, as if on cue. Henry fluttered back to the vampire's side, fretting. Octavius tried to protest as the man dabbed at his mouth with a handkerchief, but the butler's will was stronger. In the end, Octavius' shoulders sagged, and he sat there like a petulant child letting Henry have his way.

Seeing the way the vampire was acting, Turney's worries vanished. Surely, Octavius wouldn't have it in him to pout if he was seriously injured. Turney could only shake his head with a chuckle.

Scarlett's laughter joined his. "I think I'll go clean up and change while Henry is occupied."

She grabbed a set of clothes and a few bandages before leaving the room. Meanwhile, Octavius let out a whine at Henry's continued fussing.

"If you would just sit still, I'd be done already," Henry chastised. Octavius was squirming a bit, but then again, he always was.

"There," the butler stated, stepping back. "Now drink." Henry stabbed a blood bag with a straw and shoved it into Octavius' mouth—holding it in place.

Octavius glared, pouting fiercely around the straw.

Henry snorted. "You can glare all you want, but I'm not moving until you drink it all."

Octavius sighed but started to suck just as fiercely as he'd been pouting, quickly draining the blood from the bag.

Henry took the empty bag and nodded in approval. "You are as clean as you can be without bathing. I will go check on Mistress Scarlett now. Make sure to drink another bag after you clean up," the man said, with a pointed look that suggested he would be checking.

Octavius waved Henry away with a grunt, still pouting.

Turney snorted. "So, not that I'm not angry at you about the whole knocking me out thing. And we will talk about that, but first...what happened?"

Octavius' expression switched from pouting to all smiles in an instant. "Well..."

Turney listened, brows rising higher and higher as the vampire launched excitedly into details of the night. There was a lot of hand waving, and as the story continued, the vampire's gestures grew. His movements that had been stiff on arriving became more fluid—the blood appeared to be doing its job of healing him.

"And that is how the night was saved. The case was solved. And how we finally have a witch for the agency," Octavius finished, practically vibrating in his seat.

Turney sat there speechless, his brain trying to soak in all Octavius had said. "So, you saved the humans, got your asses kicked repeatedly by wraths until a good witch came and freed the demon, who then killed the bad witch. Following this, the ghost of Phoebe appeared, turned into a demon, and ran off with the original demon. And when said good witch asked if you needed help, you beyond belief offered her a job as you laid bleeding on the floor."

Octavius' smile dimmed a bit. "I mean, essentially, but I was sitting up...possibly bleeding. You also missed how the demon gave us all favors. His full name! Also, we needed a witch, and she was right there!" the vampire defended.

"Only you would try to hire someone you just met while injured." Turney huffed. "What happened next? Surely it didn't take you two hours to get back?"

Octavius crossed his arms. "We had to wait for an actual reaper to get there, and then I assisted in clearing the minds of the humans we rescued, so they could go back to their lives unaware of everything they went through."

Turney blinked. "The witch wasn't a reaper?"

"Reapers are a species of paranormal in their own right. While they do have magic of their own, they can't be anything else."

Interesting... "So, the case is solved. Now what? I'm going to be honest, you were right. It was too dangerous for me to go. But you were wrong to force the decision on me. I need to be able to trust that you aren't just going to manipulate my mind whenever you want to get your way."

And yeah, it still upset him that he'd been left behind, but how it had been done was the main issue. Turney needed to trust that Octavius wouldn't use his many abilities against him again.

Octavius frowned. "I didn't..." He trailed off, frown deepening. "I messed up, didn't I?"

"You did."

The vampire started to fidget nervously in his seat. "I'm sorry, Turney. It was wrong of me to put you to sleep. It is not an excuse, but I let my worry for your safety override logical thinking. And I failed to give you a chance to even understand my point of view. I saw a difficult conversation, and I didn't want to argue my points against what I thought was irrationality. But, my desire to avoid having a hard conversation should never have overridden your free will. You are at a disadvantage against me. We both know that. But I should have never used those advantages against you. And I promise I will not do so again."

"How about you just do your best and not make promises you may not be able to keep," Turney stated hesitantly.

Octavius frowned. "Turney, I meant what I said. I may seem fickle at times, but when I promise something, I mean it."

Turney nodded. "Fair enough."

It was the first time Octavius had not included any words similar to "try" in his promises. Turney figured there was a reason for that. "So, now what?"

The vampire grimaced before softly saying, "Now I try

to rebuild the trust I lost by my actions, and maybe redefine your job description."

Turney winced. "Octavius, I still trust you. I know you did it to keep me safe. Just don't do it again." It was the truth. He did still trust the vampire. Perhaps if he had done it to cause harm, his feelings would have been different. He blinked—wait. "What about my job description?"

Octavius perked up a bit, a small smile forming. "Well, maybe it would be better if you switched jobs with Scarlett?"

"I don't want to be your secretary. While I understand this case was too dangerous for me to actively participate, I don't see the need to change my job because of it."

The words came out quickly, and he felt shocked at his own bullshit. Had he not less than a half-hour ago had similar thoughts. That maybe this job was not suitable for him? Too dangerous for him?

"More dangerous jobs could come about," Octavius pointed out timidly.

"There could be, and we will deal with them if they do. Perhaps what could help would be involving reapers earlier, instead of at the last minute?"

Turney just barely stopped himself from laughing at his own idiocy. Even with his doubts, and the pure craziness that Octavius dragged him into, Turney found that he still wanted to keep working with him. The idea of stepping back felt wrong—that he would regret it.

"I suppose you are right. But..." Octavius fidgeted in his seat. "Could you promise me that you will be open to reason if I say something is too dangerous? I don't want to bury you, Turney." Octavius' voice trembled. "I know. I don't have much ground to stand on. I was the one who stubbornly pushed us into that house, despite something obviously being very wrong. But, please..."

Did Octavius blame himself for Turney's injuries?

"We are in this together, Octavius. I made the choice of going inside. That being said, in the future, I'll try to make the best decisions based on what you tell me. And...if you think something is too dangerous, I'll listen."

Octavius beamed happily at him. "We ARE in this together. I promise to show you I'm worthy of your trust!"

Turney held out his hand. "Partners?"

Octavius clasped his outstretched hand. "Partners."

This felt right. There was more here, more for them. Fate had led him here, hadn't it? Who was he to go against it?

Epilogue

Off Again

Turney finished dressing and stared at himself in the mirror. While the clothes were a bit stuffy, he had to admit, he looked good. His eyes drew from his fancy clothing to the freshly healed scars on his neck.

They weren't hideous, but were hard to miss. Still fresh, and deep purple in color, but nowhere near as puckered and angry looking as the scars should have been after only a single week of healing. Turney had Octavius to thank for that. The vampire's tongue had been very useful over the last week. Perhaps a bit too useful...

There were a few days that kind of blurred together, due to that skillful tongue and other parts. He chuckled at the thought.

Turney's phone buzzed in his pocket. Pulling it out, he read the text. It was from Octavius. It said *HERE* in all caps, followed by way too many emojis.

For some reason, Octavius had wanted to pick Turney up on his first official day back to work. How exactly that worked out, with him being the vampire's driver, he didn't know, but...he figured Octavius had something planned.

One last look at the scars on his neck, and Turney took off, jogging out of his room and down the stairs.

"I'm off!" he yelled out to his roommate.

"Be careful!" Alexander yelled back from somewhere inside the house.

The man had been worried after he'd come home injured. Turney wasn't sure if Alexander believed his tale of a freak bike accident or not—oh, well.

Walking out, closing the door behind him, he froze at the sight of Octavius leaning against what could only be called a classic beauty—a silver 1960 Jaguar MK II.

Octavius' arms spread out. "So, what do you think?!"

"Wow." Turney rushed over to examine the silver beauty.

"It's our new company car!" Octavius announced with a giggle. "Like it?"

While he was a speed demon, Turney loved all cars, especially classic ones. His hand caressed the shiny hood.

"She's beautiful." Unable to stop himself, he popped the hood, gasping at what he saw.

"It was originally a junker. I had someone, or rather, Henry." He nodded to the man currently in the driver's seat. "Find someone to fix it up. To update it and replace things as necessary. Like adding air conditioning and heat, not that either matter to me, but I figured it would to you."

The engine was completely boosted. Turney would have to be careful until he got a handle on how it ran. He did find Octavius' vague words on what was done endearing.

"Did I do well?" Octavius asked, sounding very proud.

While some may think making so many changes to a classic car, instead of just restoring it, was blasphemy, Turney didn't have those hang-ups. Besides, if it was initially a junker, then at least it had been repurposed. Closing the hood, he pulled Octavius to his side and gave him a peck on the cheek. "You did well."

Turney briefly wondered if the vampire realized their new ride would probably stand out just as much, or even more, than their old one did. He probably didn't—oh, well.

He'd tell him later—let him bask in his happiness for now. It's not like Octavius wouldn't eventually find out that old cars tended to draw people in like flies to a light.

Henry stepped out of the car. "If there's nothing else, I'll be off," he announced.

Turney's brow rose. "We could give you a ride." And they could because the vehicle had four seats, unlike his own car.

"Nonsense, I already called for one. You two have fun." With that, the man walked up the drive.

"Okay then..." Turney murmured.

Octavius shrugged and pulled away, getting into the passenger's seat.

Shaking his head, Turney walked around, got into the driver's side, and closed the door. The inside was a feast for his eyes. Classic dark red leather interior, with wood paneling on the dash—all brand new. He found the key was in the ignition, but the car was off.

Turning the key, he let out a groan of pleasure at the purr of the engine.

Octavius chuckled. "I'm a bit surprised to hear that sound outside the bedroom."

"Hush."

The vampire just giggled harder.

"So, where to, boss?"

"Partner!" Octavius corrected.

Turney smirked. "Where to, partner?"
"To the East Windsall Library! We have a new case!"

THE END

IF YOU ENJOYED READING all about the Undead Detective Agency, you will be pleased to know there is more to come.

READ the next books in the series now!

Book Two: Keep It Together
https://mybook.to/KeepItTogetherSR

Book Three: In Death Together
https://mybook.to/InDeathTogetherSR

Book Four: Forever Together
https://mybook.to/ForeverTogetherSR

About Shelby Rhodes

Books have always been a big part of Shelby Rhodes' life. Unfortunately, growing up writing was a constant struggle for her. So, even with her head filled with stories she never tried to write them down.

It took many years to gain the confidence to explore writing as a creative outlet. Now writing has become a way for her to dive into new adventures and explore new worlds.

With confidence, she fully intends to explore everything that has been stuck in her head. It is her hope that others will join her on her adventures.

Follow Shelby Rhodes

For upcoming releases, free shorts, or if you just want to see what I am currently working on, you can find me here:

Website:
www.shelbyrhodesauthor.com

Facebook Group:
https://www.facebook.com/groups/BeesBooksSR/

Blog:
https://shelbyrhodesauthor.blogspot.com/

Newsletter:
https://www.shelbyrhodesauthor.com/newsletter

- facebook.com/ShelbyRhode
- x.com/ShelbyRhodesAWD
- instagram.com/shelbyrhodes_author

Also By Shelby Rhodes

FAIRY TALES RETOLD

Book One: Little Red

https://mybook.to/LittleRedSR

.

VAMPIRES OF VADIN

Book One: Adrian's Bodyguard

https://mybook.to/AdriansBodyguard/

Book Two: Stephan's Monster

https://books2read.com/StephansMonster

Book Three: Sin's Thief

https://books2read.com/SinsThief

Book Four: Asher's Fire
https://books2read.com/AshersFire

THE UNDEAD DETECTIVE AGENCY

Book One: Get It Together
https://mybook.to/GetItTogether

Book Two: Keep It Together
https://mybook.to/KeepItTogetherSR

Book Three: In Death Together
https://mybook.to/InDeathTogetherSR

Book Four: Forever Together
https://mybook.to/Forever-Together

THE UNDEAD DETECTIVE FILES

Book One: Folly of Incompetence
https://mybook.to/TUDF1

THE UNWILLING ADVENTURES OF HARLOW AND FOXX

Book One: At First Irritation
https://mybook.to/AtFirstIrritation

Book Two: Taste Of Fear

https://mybook.to/TasteofFear/

Book Three: Unusual Emotions

https://mybook.to/UnusualEmotions

Book Four: Thirst Quenched

https://mybook.to/ThirstQuenched

.

CRYPTID ENFORCEMENT BUREAU

Book One: Catching a Water Nymph

https://mybook.to/ceb1

.

A LIBRARIAN'S GUIDE TO WITCHERY

Book One: A Spark of Something

https://mybook.to/lgtwitchery1

Printed in Great Britain
by Amazon